FAST ONE

FAST ONE

PAUL CAIN

VINTAGE CRIME / BLACK LIZARD
VINTAGE BOOKS · A DIVISION OF RANDOM HOUSE, INC. · NEW YORK

First Vintage Crime / Black Lizard Edition, April 1994

ISBN 0-679-75184-X
LC Number: 87-70575

Manufactured in the United States of America
10 9 8 7 6 5 4 3 2 1

Kells walked north on Spring. At Fifth he turned west, walked two blocks, turned into a small cigar store. He nodded to the squat bald man behind the counter and went through the ground-glass-paneled door into a large and bare back room.

The man sitting at a wide desk stood up, said, "Hello" heartily, went to another door and opened it, said: "Walk right in."

Kells went into a very small room, partitioned off from the other by ground-glass-paneled walls. He sat down on a worn davenport against one wall, leaned back, folded his hands over his stomach, and looked at Jack Rose.

Rose sat behind a round green-topped table, his elbows on the table, his long chin propped upon one hand. He was a dark, almost too handsome young man who had started life as Jake Rosencrancz, of Brooklyn and Queens. He said: "Did you ever hear the story about the three bears?"

Kells nodded. He sat regarding Rose gravely and nodded his head slowly up and down.

Rose was smiling. "I thought you'd have heard that one." He moved the fingers of one hand down to his ear and pulled violently at the lobe. "Now *you* tell one. Tell me the one about why you've got such a load on Kiosque in the fourth race."

Kells smiled faintly, dreamily. He said: "You don't think I'd have an inside that you'd overlooked, do you, Jakie?" He got up, stretched extravagantly and walked across the room to inspect a large map of Los Angeles County on the far wall.

Rose didn't change his position, he sat staring vacantly at the davenport. "I can throw it to Bolero."

Kells strolled back, stood beside the table. He looked at a small watch on the inside of his left wrist, said: "You might get a wire to the track, Jakie, but you couldn't reach your Eastern connections in time." He smiled with gentle irony. "Anyway, you've got the smartest book on the Coast—the smartest book west of the Mississippi, by God! You wouldn't want to take any chances with that big Beverly Hills clientele, would you?"

He turned and walked back to the davenport, sank wearily down and again folded his hands over his stomach. "What's it all about? I pick two juicy winners in a row and you squawk. What the hell do you care how many I pick?— the Syndicate's out, not you."

He slid sideways on the davenport until his head reached the armrest, pulled one long leg up to plant his foot on the seat and sprawled the other across the floor. He intently regarded a noisily spinning electric fan on a shelf in one corner. "You didn't get me out in this heat to talk about horses."

Rose wore a lightweight black felt hat. He pushed it back over his high bronzed forehead, took a cigaret out of a thin case on the table and lighted it. He said: "I'm going to reopen the *Joanna D.*—Doc Haardt and I are going to run it together—his boat, my bankroll."

Kells said: "Uh huh." He stared steadily at the electric fan, without movement or change of expression.

Rose cleared his throat, went on: "The *Joanna* used to be the only gambling barge on the Coast, but Fay moved in with the *Eaglet*, and then Max Hesse promoted a two-hundred-and-fifty-foot yacht and took the play away from both of them." Rose paused to remove a fleck of cigaret paper from his lower lip. "About three months ago, Fay and Doc got together and chased Hesse. According to the story, one of the players left a box of candy on the *Monte Carlo*— that's Hesse's boat—and along about two in the morning it exploded. No one was hurt much, but it threw an awful scare into the customers and something was said about it being a bigger and better box next time, so Hesse took a powder up the coast. But maybe you've heard all this before."

Kells looked at the fan, smiled slowly. He said: "Well—I heard it a little differently."

"You *would*." Rose mashed his cigaret out, went on: "Ev-

2

erything was okay for a couple weeks. The *Joanna* and Fay's boat were anchored about four miles apart, and their launches were running to the same wharf; but they both had men at the gangways frisking everyone who went aboard—that wasn't so good for business. Then somebody got past the protection on the *Joanna* and left another ticker. It damn near blew her in two; they beached, finally got into dry dock."

Kells said: "Uh huh."

"Tonight she goes out." Rose took another cigaret from the thin case and rolled it gently between his hand and the green baize of the table.

Kells said: "What am I supposed to do about it?"

Rose pulled the loose tobacco out of one end of the cigaret, licked the paper. "Have you got a match?"

Kells shook his head slowly.

Rose said: "Tell Fay to lay off."

Kells laughed—a long, high-pitched, sarcastic laugh.

"*Ask* him to lay off."

"Run your own errands, Jakie," Kells swung up to sit, facing Rose. "For a young fella that's supposed to be bright," he said, "you have some pretty dumb ideas."

"You're a friend of Fay's."

"Sure," Kells nodded elaborately. "Sure, I'm everybody's friend. I'm the guy they write the pal songs about." He stood up. "Is that all, Jakie?"

Rose said: "Come on out to the *Joanna* tonight."

Kells grinned. "Cut it out. You know damn well I'd never buck a house. I'm not a gambler, anyway—I'm a playboy. Stop by the hotel sometime and look at my cups."

"I mean come and look the layout over." Rose stood up and smiled carefully. "I've put in five new wheels and——"

"I've seen a wheel," Kells said. "Make mine strawberry." He turned, started toward the door.

Rose said: "I'll give you a five-percent cut."

Kells stopped, turned slowly, and came back to the table. "Cut on what?"

"The whole take, from now on."

"What for?"

"Showing three or four times a week. . . . Restoring confidence."

Kells was watching him steadily. "Whose confidence, in what?"

"Aw, nuts. Let's stop this god-damned foolishness and do some business." Rose sat down, found a paper of matches and lighted his limp cigaret. "You're supposed to be a good friend of Fay's. Whether you are or not is none of my business. The point is that everyone thinks you are, and if you show on the boat once in a while it will look like everything is under control, like Fay and I have made a deal; see?"

Kells nodded. "Why *don't* you make a deal?"

"I've been trying to reach Fay for a week." Rose tugged at the lobe of his ear. "Hell! This coast is big enough for all of us; but he won't see it. He's sore. He thinks everybody's trying to frame him."

"Everybody probably is." Kells put one hand on the table and leaned over to smile down at Rose. "Now I'll tell *you* one, Jakie. You'd like to have me on the *Joanna* because I look like the highest-powered protection at this end of the country. You'd like to carry that eighteen-carat reputation of mine around with you so you could wave it and scare all the bad little boys away."

Rose said: "All right, all right."

The phone on the table buzzed. Rose picked up the receiver, said "Yes" three times into the mouthpiece, then "All right, dear," hung up.

Kells went on: "Listen, Jakie. I don't want any part of it. I always got along pretty well by myself, and I'll keep on getting along pretty well by myself. Anyway, I wouldn't show in a deal with Doc Hardt if he was sleeping with the mayor—I hate his guts, and I'd pine away if I didn't think he hated mine."

Rose made a meaningless gesture.

Kells had straightened up. He was examining the nail of his index finger. "I came out here a few months ago with two grand and I've given it a pretty good ride. I've got a nice little joint at the Ambassador, with a built-in bar; I've got a swell bunch of telephone numbers and several thousand friends in the bank. It's a lot more fun guessing the name of a pony than guessing what the name of the next stranger I'm supposed to have shot will be. I'm having a lot of fun. I don't want any part of *anything*."

4

Rose stood up. "Okay."

Kells said: "So long, Jakie." He turned and went through the door, out through the large room, through the cigar store to the street. He walked up to Seventh and got into a cab. When they passed the big clock on the Dyas corner it was twenty minutes past three.

* * * * *

The desk clerk gave Kells several letters, and a message: *Mr. Dave Perry called at 2:35, and again at 3:25. Asked that you call him or come to his home. Important.*

Kells went to his room and put in a call to Perry. He mixed a drink and read the letters while a telephone operator called him twice to say the line was busy. When she called again, he said, "Let it go," went down and got into another cab. He told the driver: "Corner of Cherokee and Hollywood Boulevard."

Perry lived in a kind of penthouse on top of the Virginia Apartments. Kells climbed the narrow stair to the roof, knocked at the tin-sheathed fire door; he knocked again, then turned the knob, pushed the door open.

The room filled with crashing sound. Kells dropped on one knee, just inside, slammed the door shut. A strip of sunlight came in through two tall windows and yellowed the rug. Doc Haardt was lying on his back, half in, half out of the strip of sun. There was a round bluish mark on one side of his throat, and, as Kells watched, it grew larger, red.

Ruth Perry sat on a low couch against one wall and looked at Haardt's body. A door slammed some place toward the back of the house. Kells got up and turned the key in the door through which he had entered, crossed quickly and stood above the body.

Haardt had been a big loose-jowled Dutchman with a mouthful of gold. His dead face looked as if he were about to drawl: "Well . . . I'll tell you . . ." A small automatic lay on the floor near his feet.

Ruth Perry stood up and started to scream. Kells put one hand on the back of her neck, the other over her mouth. She took a step forward, put her arms around his body. She looked up at him and he took his hand away from her mouth.

"Darling! I thought he was going to get *you*." She spoke

5

very rapidly. Her face was twisted with fear. "He was here an hour. He made Dave call you. . . ."

Kells patted her cheek. "Who, baby?"

"I don't know." She was coming around. "A nance. A little guy with glasses."

Kells inclined his head toward Haardt's body, asked: "What about Doc?"

"He came up about two-thirty. . . . Said he had to see you and didn't want to go to the hotel. Dave called you and left word. Then about an hour ago that little son of a bitch walked in and told us all to sit down on the floor. . . ."

Someone pounded heavily on the door.

They tiptoed across to a small, curtained archway that led to the dining room. Just inside the archway Dave Perry lay on his stomach.

Ruth Perry said: "The little guy slugged Dave when he made a pass for the phone, after he called you. He came to, a while ago, and the little guy let him have it again. What a boy!"

Someone pounded on the door again and the sound of loud voices came through faintly.

Kells said: "I'm a cinch for this one if they find me here. That's what the plant was for." He nodded toward the door. "Can they get around to the kitchen?"

"Not unless they go down and come up the fire escape. That's the way our boy friend went."

"I'll go the other way." Kells went swiftly to Haardt's body, knelt and picked up the automatic. "I'll take this along to make your story good. Stick to it, except the calls to me and the reason Doc was here."

Ruth Perry nodded. Her eyes were shiny with excitement.

Kells said: "I'll see what I can get on the pansy—and try to talk a little sense to the telephone girl at the hotel and the cab driver that had led me here."

The pounding on the door was almost continuous. Someone put a heavy shoulder to it, the hinges creaked.

Kells started toward the bedroom, then turned and came back. She tilted her mouth up to him and he kissed her. "Don't let this lug husband of yours talk," he said—jerked his head down at Dave Perry—"and maybe you'd better go

6

into a swoon to alibi not answering the door. Let 'em bust it in."

"My God, Gerry! I'm too excited to faint."

Kells kissed her again, lightly. He brought one arm up stiffly, swiftly from his side; the palm down, the fist loosely clinched. His knuckles smacked sharply against her chin. He caught her body in his arms, went into the living room and laid her gently on the floor. Then he took out his handkerchief, carefully wiped the little automatic, and put it on the floor midway between Haardt, Perry and Ruth Perry.

He went into the bedroom and into the adjoining bathroom. He raised the window and squeezed through to a narrow ledge. He was screened from the street by part of the building next door, and from the alley by a tree that spread over the back yard of the apartment house. A few feet along the ledge he felt with his foot for a steel rung, found it, swung down to the next, across a short space to the sill of an open corridor-window of the next-door building.

He walked down the corridor, down several flights of stairs and out a rear door of the building. Down a kind of alley he went through a wooden gate into a bungalow court and through to Whitley and walked north.

* * * * *

Cullen's house was on the northeastern slope of Whitley Heights, a little way off Cahuenga. He answered the fourth ring, stood in the doorway blinking at Kells. "Well, stranger. Long time no see."

Cullen was a heavily built man of about forty-five. He had a round pale face, a blue chin and blue-black hair. He was naked except for a pair of yellow silk pajama trousers; a full-rigged ship was elaborately tattooed across his wide chest.

Kells said: "H'are ya, Willie," went past Cullen into the room. He sat down in a deep leather chair, took off his Panama hat and ran his fingers through red, faintly graying hair.

Cullen went into the kitchen and came back with tall glasses, a bowl of ice and a squat bottle.

Kells said: "Well, Willie—"

Cullen held up his hand. "Wait. Don't tell me. Make me guess." He closed his eyes, went through the motions of mystic communion, then opened his eyes, sat down and poured two drinks. "You're in another jam," he said.

Kells twisted his mouth into a wholly mirthless smile, nodded. "You're a genius, Willie." He sipped his drink, leaned back.

Cullen sat down.

Kells said: "You know Max Hesse pretty well. You've been out to his house in Flintridge."

"Sure."

"Do you know what Dave Perry looks like?"

"No."

Kells put his glass down. "A little patent-leather, pop-eyed guy with a waxed mustache. Wears gray silk shirts with tricky brocaded stripes. Used to run a string of trucks down from Frisco—had some kind of warehouse connection up there. Stood a bad rap on some forged Liberty Bonds about a year ago and went broke beating it. Married Grant Fay's sister when he was on top."

"I've seen her," Cullen said. "Nice dish."

"You've never seen Dave at Hesse's?"

Cullen shook his head. "I don't think so."

"All right. It wouldn't mean a hell of a lot, anyway." Kells picked up his glass, drained it, stood up. "I want to use the phone."

He dialed a number printed in large letters on the cover of the telephone book, asked for the Reporters' Room. When the connection was made, he asked for Shep Beery, spoke evenly into the instrument: "Listen, Shep, this is Gerry. In a little while you'll probably have some news for me. . . . Yeah. . . . Call Granite six five one six. . . . And Shep—who copped in the fourth race at Juana? . . . Thanks, Shep. Got the number? . . . OK."

Cullen was pouring drinks. "If all this is as bad as you're making it look—you have a very trusting nature," he observed.

Kells was dialing another number. He said, over his shoulder: "I win twenty-four hundred on Kiosque."

"That's fine."

"Perry shot Doc Haardt to death about four o'clock."

8

"That's fine. Where were you?" Cullen was stirring his drink.

Kells jiggled the hook up and down. "Goddamn telephones," he said. He dialed the number again, then turned his head to smile at Cullen. "I was here."

The telephone clicked. Kells turned to it, asked: "Is Number Four on duty?" There was a momentary wait, then: "Hello, Stella? This is Mister Kells . . . Listen, Stella, there weren't any calls for me between two and four today. . . . I know it's on the record, baby, but I want it off. Will you see what you can do about it? . . . Right away? . . . That's fine. And Stella, the number I called about three-thirty—the one where the line was busy . . . Yes. That was Granite six five one six. . . . Got it? . . . All right, kid, I'll tell you all about it later. 'Bye."

Cullen said: "As I was saying—you have a very trusting nature."

Kells was riffling the pages of a small blue address book. "One more," he said, mostly to himself. He spun the dial again. "Hello—Yellow? Ambassador stand, please. . . . Hello. Is Fifty-eight in? . . . That's the little bald-headed Mick, isn't it? . . . No, no: *Mick*. . . . Sure . . . Send him to two eight nine Iris Circle when he gets in. . . . Two . . . eight . . . nine . . . That's in Hollywood; off Cahuenga. . . ."

They sat for several minutes without speaking. Kells sipped at his drink and stared out of the window. Then he said: "I'm not putting on an act for you, Willie. I don't know how to tell it; it doesn't make much sense, yet." He smiled lazily at Cullen. "Are you good at riddles?"

"Terrible."

The phone rang. Cullen got up to answer it.

Kells said: "Maybe that's the answer."

Cullen called him to the phone. He said, "Yes, Shep," and was silent a little while. Then he said, "Thanks," hung up and went back to the deep leather chair. "I guess maybe we can't play it the way I'd figured," he said. "There's a tag out for me."

Cullen said slowly, sarcastically: "My pal! They'll trace the phony call that your girl friend Stella's handling, or get to the cab driver before he gets to you. We'll have a couple

9

carloads of law here in about fifteen minutes."

"That's all right, Willie. You can talk to 'em."

Cullen grinned mirthlessly. "I haven't spoken to a copper for four years."

Kells straightened in his chair. "Listen. Doc went to Perry's to see me. . . . What for? I was with Jack Rose being propositioned to come in with him and Doc, on the *Joanna*. They're evidently figuring Fay or Hesse to make things tough and wanted me for a flash."

He looked at his watch. Cullen was stirring ice into another drink.

Kells went on, swiftly: "When I open the door at Perry's, somebody lets Doc have it and goes out through the kitchen. Maybe. The back door slammed but it might have been the draft when I opened the front door. Dave is cold with an egg over his ear and Ruth Perry says that a little queen with glasses shot Doc and sapped Dave when he spoke out of turn. . . ."

Cullen said: "You're not making this up as you go along, are you?"

Kells paid no attention to Cullen's interruption. "The rod is on the floor. I tell Ruth to stick to her story. . . ."

Cullen raised one eyebrow, smiled faintly with his lips.

Kells said, "She *will*," went on: ". . . and try to keep Dave quiet while I figure an alibi, try to find out what it's all about. I smack her to make it look good and then I get the bright idea that if I leave the gun there they'll hold both of them, no matter what story they tell. They'd *have* to hold somebody; Doc had a lot of friends downtown."

Kells finished his drink, picked up his hat and put it on. "I figured Ruth to office Dave that I was working on it and that he might keep his mouth shut if he wasn't in on the plant."

Cullen sighed heavily.

Kells said: "He *was*. Shep tells me that Dave says I had an argument with Doc, shot him, and clipped Dave when he tried to stop me. Shep can't get a line on Ruth's story, but I'll lay six, two, and even that she's still telling the one about the little guy." He stood up. "They're both being held *incommunicado*. And here's one for the book: Reilly made the pinch. Now what the hell was Reilly doing out here if it wasn't tipped?"

Cullen said: "It's a set-up. It was the girl."

Kells shook his head slowly.

"Dave knows it and is trying to cover for her," Cullen went on. "She told you a fast one about the little guy and I'll bet she's telling the same story as Dave right now."

"Wrong."

Cullen laughed. "If you didn't think it was possible you wouldn't look that way."

"You're crazy. If she wanted to frame me she wouldn't've put on that act. She wouldn't've . . ."

"Oh, yes, she would. She'd let you go and put the finger on you from a distance." Cullen scratched his side, under the arm, yawned.

Kells said: "What about Dave?"

"Maybe Doc socked Dave."

"She'd cheer."

"Maybe." Cullen got up and walked to a window. "Maybe she cheered and squeezed the heater at the same time. That's been done, you know."

Kells shook his head. "I don't see it," he said. "There are too many other angles."

"You wouldn't see it." Cullen turned from the window, grinned. "You don't know anything about feminine psychology.

Kells said: "I invented it."

Cullen spread his mouth into a wide thin line, nodded ponderously. "Sure," he said, "there are a lot of boys sitting up in Quentin counting their fingers who invented it too." He walked to the stair and back. "Anyway, you had a pretty good hunch when you left Exhibit A on the floor."

"I'm superstitious. I haven't carried a gun for over a year." Kells smiled a little.

Cullen said: "Another angle—she's Fay's sister."

"That's swell, but it doesn't mean anything."

"It might." Cullen yawned again extravagantly, scratched his arms.

Kells asked: "Yen?"

"Uh huh. I was about to cook up a couple loads when you busted in with all this heavy drama." Cullen jerked his head toward the stair. "Eileen is upstairs."

Kells said: "I thought the last cure took."

"Sure. It took." Cullen smiled sleepily. "Like the other nine. I'm down to two, three pipes each other day."

They looked at one another expressionlessly for a little while.

A car chugged up the short curving slope below the front door, stopped. Kells turned and went into the semidarkness of the kitchen. A buzzer whirred. Cullen went to the front door, opened it, said: "Come in." A little Irishman in the uniform of a cab driver came into the room and took off his hat. Cullen went back to the chair and sat down with his back to the room, picked up his drink.

The phone rang.

Kells came out of the kitchen and answered it. He stood for a while staring vacantly at the cab driver, then said, "Thanks, kid," hung up, put his hand in his pocket and took out a small neatly folded sheaf of bills. "When you brought me here from the hotel about four o'clock," he said, "I forgot to tip you." He peeled off two bills and held them toward the driver.

The little man came forward, took the bills and examined them. One was a hundred, the other a fifty. "Do I have to tell it in court?" he asked.

Kells smiled, shook his head. "You probably won't have to tell it anywhere."

The driver said: "Thank you very much, sir." He went to the door and put on his hat.

Kells said: "Wait a minute." He spoke to Cullen: "Can I use your heap, Willie?"

Cullen nodded without enthusiasm, without turning his head.

Kells turned to the driver. "All right, Paddy. You'd better stall for an hour or so. Then if anyone asks you anything, you can tell 'em you picked me up here—on this last trip— and hauled me down to Malibu. No house number—just the gas station, or something."

The driver said, "Right," went out.

"Our high-pressure police department finally got around to Stella." Kells went back to his chair, sat down on the edge of it and grinned cheerfully at Cullen. "How much cash have you got, Willie?" Cullen gazed tragically at the ceiling.

"It was too late to catch the bank," Kells went on, "and

it's a cinch I can't get within a mile of it in the morning. They'll have it loaded."

"I get a break. I've only got about thirty dollars."

Kells laughed. "You'd better keep that for cigarets. I've got to square this thing pronto and it'll probably take better than change—or maybe I'll take a little trip." He got up, walked across the room and studied his long white face in a mirror. He leaned forward, rubbed two fingers of one hand lightly over his chin. "I wonder if I'd like Mexico."

Cullen didn't say anything.

Kells turned from the mirror. "I guess I'll have to take a chance on reaching Rose and picking up my twenty-four C's."

Cullen said. "That'll be a lot of fun."

* * * * *

The first street lights and electric signs were being turned on when Kells parked on Fourth Street between Broadway and Hill. He walked up Hill to Fifth, turned into a corner building, climbed stairs to the third floor and walked down the corridor to a window on the Fifth Street side. He stood there for several minutes intently watching the passersby on the sidewalk across the street. Then he went back to the car.

As he pressed the starter, a young chubby-faced patrolman came across the street and put one foot on the running board, one hand on top of the door. "Don't you know you can't park here between four and six?" he said.

Kells glanced at his watch. It was five thirty-five. He said: "No. I'm a stranger here."

"Let's see your driver's license."

Kells smiled, said evenly: "I haven't got it with me."

The patrolman shook his head sadly. "Where you from?" he asked.

"San Francisco."

"You're in the big city now, buddy." The patrolman sneered at Kells, the car, the sky. He seemed lost in thought for a half-minute, then he said: "All right. Now you know."

Kells drove up Fourth to the top of the hill. His eyes were half closed and there was an almost tender expression on his face. He swore softly, continuously, obscenely. His anger had

13

worn itself out by the time he had parked the car on Grand and walked down the steep hill to the rear entrance of the Biltmore. He got off the elevator at the ninth floor, walked past the questioning stare of the woman at the key desk, down a long hall, knocked at the door of Suite 9D.

Rose opened the door. He stood silently, motionlessly for perhaps five seconds, then he ran his tongue over his lower lip and said: "Come in."

Kells went into the room.

A husky, pale eyed young man was straddling a small chair, his elbows on the back of it, his chin between his hands. His sand-colored hair was carefully combed down over one side of his forehead. His mouth hung a little open and he breathed through it regularly, audibly.

Rose said: "This is Mister O'Donnell of Kansas City . . . Mister Kells."

The young man stood up, still straddling the chair, held out a pink hand. "Glad t' know you."

Kells shook his hand cursorily, said: "I stopped by for my dough.

"Sure." Rose went to a cabinet and took out a bottle of whiskey and three glasses. "Why didn't you pick it up at the store?"

Kells walked across the room and sat down on the arm of a big, heavily upholstered chair. O'Donnell was in his shirtsleeves. O'Donnell's coat was lying across a table, back and a little to one side of Kells.

Kells said: "I want it in cash."

Rose put the bottle and glasses down on a wide central table. "I haven't got any cash here," he said, "we'll have to go over to the store." He went toward the telephone on a desk against one wall. "I'll order some White Rock."

Kells said: "No."

Rose stopped, turned—he was smiling. O'Donnell unstraddled the chair and sauntered in Kells' general direction. His pale eyes were fixed blankly on Kells' stomach. Kells stood up very straight, took two long swift sidewise steps and grabbed O'Donnell's coat. The automatic in a shoulder holster which had been under the coat clattered to the floor. O'Donnell dived for it and Kells stamped hard on his fingers, brought his right knee up hard into O'Donnell's

14

face. O'Donnell grunted, lost his balance and fell over backward; he rolled back and forth silently, holding both hands over his nose.

Rose was standing by the central table, holding the whiskey bottle by the neck. He was still smiling as if that expression had hardened, congealed on his face.

Kells stooped and scooped up the gun.

There was a wide double door at one side of the room, leading to a bedroom, and beyond, directly across the bedroom, there was another door leading to a bath. It opened and a very blonde woman stuck her head out. She called: "What's the matter, Jack?"

Kells could see her reflected indistinctly in one of the mirrors of the wide double door. He and O'Donnell were out of her line of vision.

Rose said: "Nothing, honey." He tipped the bottle, poured a drink.

"Is Lou here yet?" She raised her voice above the sound of water running in the tub.

"No."

The blonde woman closed the door. O'Donnell sat up and took out a handkerchief and held it over his nose.

Kells said: "Now . . ."

Rose shook his head slowly. "I've got about a hundred an' ten."

Kells rubbed the corner of one of his eyes with his middle finger. He said: "All right, Jakie. I want you to call the shop, and I want you to say 'Hello, Frank?'—and if it isn't Frank I want you to wait till Frank comes to the phone, and then I want you to say 'Bring three thousand dollars over to the hotel right away.' Then I want you to hang up."

Rose picked up the glass and drank. "There isn't more than four hundred dollars at the store," he said. "It's all down on the *Joanna*—for the opening."

Kells looked at him thoughtfully for a little while. "All right. Get your hat."

Rose hesitated a moment, looked down at O'Donnell, then walked over to a chair near the bedroom door and picked up his hat.

Kells said: "Now, Jakie, *back* into the bedroom." Kells transferred the automatic to his left hand, took hold the back of O'Donnell's collar with his right, said, "Pardon me, Mister O'Donnell."

He dragged O'Donnell across the floor to the bedroom door—keeping Rose in front of him—across the bedroom floor to the bathroom. He opened the bathroom door, jerked O'Donnell to his feet and shoved him inside. The blonde woman in the tub screamed once. Then Kells took the key from the inside of the door, slammed the door, cutting the sound of her second scream to a thin cry, locked it.

Rose was standing at the foot of one of the twin beds. The dark skin was drawn very tightly over his jaw muscles. He looked very sick.

Kells put the key in his pocket. He grinned, said: "Come on."

They walked together to the outer door of the suite. Kells lifted one point of his vest, stuck the automatic inside the waistband of his trousers. He let his belt out a notch or so until the gun nestled as comfortably and as securely as possible beneath his ribs, then pulled the point of his vest down over the butt. It made only a slight bulge against the narrowness of his waist. He said: "Jakie, have you any idea how fast I can get it out and how well I can use it?"

Rose didn't say anything. He ran the fingers of one hand down over the left side of his face and looked at the floor.

Kells went on: "I've been framed for one caper today and I don't intend to be framed for another. The next one'll be bona fide—and I'd just as soon it'd be you, and I'd just as soon it'd be in the lobby of the Biltmore as any place else." He opened the door and switched out the light. "Let's go."

They went down in the elevator, out through the Galleria to Fifth Street and up the south side of the street to Grand, walked up the steep hill to the car.

Kells said: "You'd better drive Jake. I haven't got a license."

Rose said he didn't have a license either.

*   *   *   *   *

Rose drove. They went up Grand to Tenth, over Tenth to Main. When they turned into Main, headed south, Kells twisted around in the seat until he was almost facing Rose. Kells' hands were lying idly in his lap. He said: "Who shot Doc?"

16

Rose turned his head for a second, smiled a little. "President Roosevelt."

Kells licked his lips. "Who shot Doc, Jakie?"

Rose kept his eyes straight ahead. He turned his long chin a fraction of an inch towards Kells, spoke gently, barely moving his mouth: "Perry and the D A and all the papers say *you* did. That's good enough for me."

Kells chuckled. He said: "Step on it. Your chum from Kansas City won't stay locked up forever." He watched the needle of the speedometer quiver from twenty-five to thirty-five. "That'll do."

They went out Main to Slauson, east to Truck Boulevard, south.

Kells said: "You're a swell driver, Jakie—you should've stayed in the hack racket back in Brooklyn." He looked at the slowly darkening sky, went on, as if to himself: "There must be a very tricky inside on this play. The rake-off on all the boats together wouldn't be worth all his finaygling— shootings and pineapples and what have you." He turned slowly, soft-eyed toward Rose. "What's it all about?'"

Rose was silent. He twisted his lips up at the corners.

As they neared the P & O wharf where the *Joanna* motor launches tied up, Kells said: "You look a lot more comfortable now that you're getting near the home grounds. But remember, Jakie—one word out of turn, one wrong move, and you get it right in the belly. I'm just dippy enough to do it. I get mad when a goose tries to run out on me."

They left the car in a parking station, walked down the wharf. It was too early for customers. A few crap and blackjack dealers, waiters, one floor man whom Kells knew slightly were lounging about the small waiting room, waiting for the first boat to leave. They all stopped talking when Kells and Rose went into the waiting room.

The floor man said, "Hello, boss," to Rose, nodded to Kells.

Rose said: "Let's go."

The man who owned the launches came out of his little office. He said: "Mickey ain't here yet. He makes the first trip."

Rose looked away from him, said: "Take us out yourself."

The man nodded doubtfully, locked the office door and

went out toward the small float where the four boats that ran to the *Joanna* were tied up. The dealers and waiters got up and followed him. The floor man lagged behind. He acted as if he wanted to talk to Rose.

Kells took Rose's arm. "Let's go over here a minute, first," he said.

They crossed the wharf to where one of the *Eaglet* launches was moored at the foot of a short gangway. A big red-faced man was working on the engine.

Kells called to him: "Has Fay gone aboard yet?"

The man straightened up, nodded. "He went out about six o'clock."

Kells said: "You go out and tell Fay that Kells sent you. Tell him I'm going aboard the *Joanna* to collect some money. Tell him to send some of the boys with you, and you come back and circle around the *Joanna* until I hail you to pick me up. Got it?"

The red-faced man said: "Yes, sir—but we're expecting quite a crowd tonight—and one of the boats is out of commission."

Kells said: "That's all right—one boat can handle the crowd. This is important." He grinned at Rose: "Isn't it, Jakie?"

Rose smiled with his mouth; his eyes were very cold and far-away.

The red-faced man said: "All right, Mister Kells." He spun the crank, and when the engine was running he put the big aluminum cover over it, cast off the lines and went to the wheel.

Kells and Rose went across the wharf and down onto the float and aboard the *Joanna* launch. A helper cast off the lines and the launch stood out through the narrows, down the bay.

Darkness came over the water swiftly.

They rounded the breakwater, headed toward a distant twinkling light. One of the dealers talked in a low voice to the man at the wheel; two of the waiters chattered to each other in Italian. The others were silent.

In the thirty-five or forty minutes that it took to come up to the *Joanna*, the wind freshened and the launch slid up and down over the long smooth swells. The lights of the *Joanna* came out of the darkness through thin ribbons of fog.

Kells walked up the gangway a step behind and a little to the left of Rose. Several seamen and hangers-on stood at the rail, stared at them. They crossed the cabaret that had been built across the upper deck, went down a wide red-carpeted stairway to the principal gambling room. It ran the width and nearly the length of the ship. Dozens of green-covered tables lined the sides: Blackjack, chuck-a-luck, faro, roulette, crap. Two dealers were removing the canvas covers from one of the big roulette tables.

They turned at the bottom of the stairs and went aft to a white athwartship bulkhead. There were three doors in the bulkhead; the middle one was ajar. They went in.

Swanstrom sat in a tilted swivel chair at a large roll-top desk. Swanstrom had been Doc Haardt's house manager; he was a very fat man with big brown eyes, a slow and eager smile. A black-and-white kitten was curled up on his lap.

The swivel chair creaked as he swung heavily forward and stood up. He put the kitten on the desk, said: "How are ya, Jack?"

Rose nodded abstractedly, cleared his throat. "This is Mister Kells. . . . Mister Swanstrom."

Swanstrom opened his mouth. He held out his hand toward Kells and looked at the door. Kells had stopped just inside the door; he half turned and closed it, pressed the little brass knob and the spring lock clicked. He stood looking at Rose, Swanstrom, the room.

There was a blue-shaded drop light hanging from the center of the overhead and another over the desk. There was a big old-fashioned safe against one wall, and beside it there was a short ladder leading up to a narrow shoulder-height platform that ran across all the forward bulkhead—the one through which they had entered. The bulkhead above the platform was lined with sheet iron and there was a two-inch slit running across it at about the height of a medium sized man's eyes. There were two .30-.30 rifles on the platform, leaning against the bulkhead. There was another narrow door back of the desk.

Rose went to the desk and sat down, took a gray leather key case out of his pocket and unlocked one of the desk drawers. He slid the drawer open and took out a cigar box

19

and opened it, took out a sheaf of hundred-dollar notes, slid the rubber band off onto two fingers and counted out twenty-four. He put the rest back in the box, the box back in the drawer, locked it. He counted the money again and held it out toward Kells. "Now, if you'll give me a receipt . . ." he said.

Kells took the money and tucked it into his inside breast pocket, said: "Sure. Write it out." His face was hard and expressionless.

Rose scribbled a few words on a piece of paper and Kells went to the desk and leaned over and signed it.

Swanstrom was still standing in the middle of the room looking self-consciously at Kells, a meaningless smile curving his mouth. He said: "Well, I guess I better go up and see if everything's ready for the first load."

Kells said: "We'll all go."

There was silence for a moment and then a new thin voice lisped: "Please lock your hands together back of your neck."

Kells slowly turned his head and looked at the narrow white door behind the desk. It had been opened about three inches and the slim blue barrel of a heavy-caliber revolver was through the opening. As he watched, the door swung open a little farther and he saw a little dark man standing in the dimness of the passageway. The little man was leaning against the side of the passageway and holding the revolver pointed at Kells' chest and smiling through thick-lensed glasses.

Kells put his hands back of his neck.

Rose came around the desk and took the automatic out of Kells' belt, held it by the barrel and swung it swiftly back and then forward at Kells' head. Kells moved his hand enough to take most of the butt of the automatic on his knuckles, and bent his knees and grabbed Rose's arm. Then he fell backwards, pulled Rose down with him.

The little man came into the room quickly and kicked the side of Kells' head very hard. Kells relaxed his grip on Rose and Rose stood up, brushed himself off and went over and kicked Kells very carefully, drawing his foot back and aiming, and then kicking very accurately and hard.

The kitten jumped off the desk and went to Kells' bloody

head and sniffed delicately. Kells could feel the kitten's warm breath. Then everything got dark and he couldn't feel anything any more.

2

There was very dim yellow light coming from somewhere. There were voices. One was O'Donnell's voice but it was from too far off to make out the words. Then the voices went away.

Kells moved his shoulder an inch at a time and turned his head slowly. It felt as if it might fall in several pieces. He closed his eyes. The yellow light was coming through a partially opened door at the other end of a long dark storeroom. Kells could dimly see cases piled along the sides: He could see a man sitting on one of the cases, silhouetted against the pale light.

The man stood up and came over and looked down at him. Kells closed his eyes and lay very still and the man walked back and sat down and put his elbows on his knees, his chin in his hands. There was thin jazz music coming from somewhere above; the man tapped his foot, in time.

Kells watched him for a long time; then the man got up and came over again and lighted a match and held it down near his face. He went away through the door and closed it behind him. In the moment that the door was open Kells saw that the room was very big, and rounded at the end opposite the door—following the line of the ship's stern. There were hundreds of cases piled along the sides. Then the door closed and it was dark.

Kells got up slowly, holding his head between his hands, took out a handkerchief and tried to wipe some of the dried blood from his face. He went swiftly to the door, found it locked. He leaned against the bulkhead, and sharp buzzing hammers pounded inside his skull.

In a little while he heard the man coming back. He stood flat against the bulkhead just inside the door, and when the man came in Kells slid one arm around his neck and pulled it tight with his other hand. The man's curse was cut to a

21

faint gurgle; they fell down and rolled across the deck. Kells kept his arm pressed tightly against the man's throat and after a time he stopped struggling, went limp. Kells lay panting beside him for a few minutes without releasing his hold and then, when he was sure that the man was unconscious, got up. He stooped and fumbled in the man's pockets, found a box of matches and a small woven-leather blackjack.

He went swiftly to the door, through to a narrow L-shaped room where unused chairs, stools, tables were stored. There was a hatchway with a steep-sloped stair leading down to another compartment. Kells went quietly down.

There was a paper-shaded light over the flat desk; there were two bunks. A man in overalls was snoring in one. There was a watertight door in one bulkhead and Kells went through it to a dark passageway that led forward along the ship's side. About thirty feet along the passageway he stepped on something soft, yielding; he lighted a match and held it down to the drained face of the little man who had said "Please lock your hands together back of your neck." There was a dark stain high on the front of his shirt; the heavy blue revolver was gripped in his outstretched hand. He was breathing.

Kells pried the revolver out of the little man's hand and stood up. He balanced the revolver across his fingers and a kind of soft insanity came into his eyes. He shook out the match and went back along the dark passageway, through the compartment where the overalled man was sleeping, up to the L-shaped storeroom. In the far end of the L there was another narrow door. Kells swung it open softly.

Swanstrom was sitting at the desk with his back to the door. Another man, a spare thin-haired consumptive-looking man was sitting on a chair on the platform, one of the .30-.30's across his knees. He looked at Kells and he looked at the big blue revolver in Kells' hand and he put the .30-.30 down on the platform.

Swanstrom swung around and opened his mouth, and then he smiled as if he were very tired.

Kells said: "Twenty-four hundred, and goddamned quick."

The thin moan of saxophones came down to them from somewhere above.

Swanstrom inclined his head toward the desk. He said, still with the tired smile: "I ain't got a key."

The lock of the other door clicked and the door opened and Rose and O'Donnell came in. They stood still for perhaps five seconds; O'Donnell was almost behind Rose. He closed the door and then he reached for the light-switch on the bulkhead. Kells squeezed the big Colt; O'Donnell fell forward to his hands and knees, shook his head slowly from side to side, sank down and forward onto his face.

Most of Kells' face was dark with dried blood. His eyes were glazed, insane. He said: "Anybody else?"

He swayed. He moved slowly toward Rose. Swanstrom was staring at O'Donnell; Swanstrom stood up, and in the same instant someone knocked heavily on the door, the knob rattled. Someone shouted outside. Kells moved toward Rose. His cold eyes and the slim blue barrel of the revolver were focused on Rose's belt buckle.

Rose licked his full lower lip, and sweat glistened on his dark forehead. He put one hand into his inside pocket and took out the folded sheaf of hundred-dollar notes, held them towards Kells.

Kells took them, nodded. He grinned, and the grin was a terrible thing on his bloody face. He backed slowly, carefully to the door through which he had entered, said, "First man through gets one in the guts," backed out and closed the door.

He went swiftly to the hatchway, down. The man who had been asleep had gone. Kells went through the passageway to the little man, lighted a match and saw that he was conscious. His eyes were open behind the thick glasses and he smiled up at the flare of the match, kicked viciously at Kells' knee.

Kells said: "Now, now—Garbo."

He gripped the little man by the collar and dragged him along the passageway. There was sudden faint light at the after end and he waited until a shadow came into the light, shot at it once, twice. The sound was like thunder in the narrow space.

They went on laboriously, Kells dragging the little man,

the little man cursing him softly, savagely. The after end of the passageway was dark now. Kells sucked in breath sharply. There was acrid smoke in the darkness—something more than the smell of black powder. It was like burning wood. Kells pressed his body against the bulkhead, risked another match.

A little way ahead there was a large rectangular port—a coaling port—in the ship's side, another on the inboard side of the passageway. The match flickered out and Kells edged forward, felt in the darkness for the big iron clamps. They were stiff from disuse but he strained and tugged until all but one were unscrewed, laid back. The last he hammered with the butt of the revolver until it gave; thrust all his weight against the plate. It creaked, swung slowly outward.

The sea was black, oily. The fog had thinned a little and the ship rolled lazily on a long even ground swell. Far to the left, Kells could see yellow sky over Long Beach, and to the right a distant winking light that might be the *Eaglet*. There was no sign of the launch.

Then he heard shouting and the sound of people running on the deck above him. He waited, listened, looked at the sea. The black water reddened; Kells leaned far out of the port and saw a long tongue of flame astern. As he watched, the water and the sky brightened. All the after quarter of the ship was afire.

When he again looked forward, a launch had rounded the bow, was idling about two hundred yards off.

Kells stuck the revolver in his belt, untied and kicked off his shoes. Then he took out the revolver, fired three into the red darkness. By the mounting glow from astern he thought he saw a white hand raised; the launch swung toward him in a wide circle.

He put the sheaf of crisp bills into his hip pocket, buttoned the flap. He took off his coat and threw it and the revolver into the sea. He picked the little man up in his arms, said, "Pull yourself together, baby—we're going byebye," got him somehow through the port, dropped him. Then he stood on the lower edge of the port, took a deep breath, dived. There was darkness and the shock of cold water.

He came to the surface a few yards from the little man, reached him in two long strokes and hooked one hand under his armpit. The shock had revived him—he struggled feebly.

Kells grunted, "Take it easy," and swam toward the launch.

The red-faced man whom Kells had talked to on the wharf leaned over the gunwale; together they hoisted the little man aboard. Then the red-faced man helped Kells. He had been alone in the launch. He went to the wheel.

Kells took off his trousers and wrung them out. He said: "How come you're alone?"

The red-faced man put his wheel hard over, spat high into the wind. "Fay said for you to go something yourself," he said. "I went back to the wharf and then I got to worrying, so I come out by myself."

Kells squatted beside the little man, looked back at the *Joanna*. Her after third was an up-and-down pillar of flame.

"Looks like a fire to me," he said. He looked down at the white, drawn face. "You've been playing with matches."

The little man smiled.

"It's a fire, sure enough." The red-faced man touched the throttle. Then he added: "There ain't much of a crowd. They'll all have a lifeboat apiece." He chuckled to himself. "You're pretty wet—where do you want to go?"

Kells said: "*Eaglet*." He put on his pants.

* * * * *

Fay sat in a big chair behind a desk. He was a very big, powerfully muscled man with straight black hair, a straight nose, empty ice-gray eyes.

There was a woman. She sat on one side of the desk with a large glass in her hand. She was very drunk—but in a masculine way.

Kells stood across from Fay. His expression was not pleasant. He said: "What's it all about? Were you trying to get me killed?"

Fay said: "Why not?"

The woman giggled softly.

Fay turned his head without changing his blank expression, looked at the little man who had been carried into the cabin, laid on a couch. "Who's your boy friend?"

The woman said: "Nemo Kastner of K C—little Nemo, the chorus boys' delight."

Kells looked at the woman. She was blonde—but darkly, warmly. Her mouth was very red without a great deal of rouge, and her eyes were shadowed and deep. She was a tall woman with very interesting curves.

Fay said: "This is Miss Granquist."

Kells nodded shortly. He took a bottle and a glass from the desk, went to the little man.

Fay got up and went to one of the ports. He looked out at the *Joanna*, spur of fire against the horizon. "Beautiful!" he said—"beautiful!" Then he turned and went over to where Kells knelt over little Kastner.

Kells held a glass of whiskey to Kastner's mouth. Kastner drank as if he wanted it very much.

Kells looked up at Fay. He dipped his head toward Kastner, said: "This is the young fella who rubbed Doc."

Fay twisted his mouth to a slow sneer. His eyes dulled. He said: "*You* shot Doc, you son of a bitch—and tried to hang it on Ruth."

Kells stood up slowly.

Kastner laughed quietly, carefully, as though it hurt his chest. "God almighty!" he said—"what a bunch of suckers." His lisp was soft, slight.

Kells and Fay stood looking at one another for a little while. Then the woman said: "You'd better get a doctor for his nibs." She was sitting with her elbows on the desk, holding her face tightly between her hands.

Kastner shook his head. He laughed again as though moved by some secret, uncontrollable mirth. There was a little blood on his mouth.

Kells said: "You want a drink." He poured more whiskey into the glass and sat down beside Kastner.

"What a bunch of suckers!" Kastner looked at the glass of whiskey. He looked at and through Kells. "Rose called Eddie O'Donnell and me after you left him this afternoon. He said Dave Perry had called while you were there—told him that Doc was at the joint in Hollywood waiting for you. . . ."

Kells held the glass to Kastner's mouth. He drank, closed his eyes for a moment, went on: "Perry knew Rose was going to have Doc bumped—an' he knew Rose wanted to frame it for you. Only he'd figured on doing it on the boat. It looked like a good play."

Kells said: "Why me?"

Kastner coughed and held one hand very tightly against his chest. "Rose thinks you're a wrong guy to be on somebody else's side—an' he wanted to tie it up to Fay."

Kastner's dark, near-sighted eyes wandered for a moment to Fay. "Rose figures on airing everybody he ain't sure of—he's got a list. That's why he sent for Eddie an' me. He wants to move in on the whole town—him and Dave Perry and Reilly."

Kastner stopped, closed his eyes. Then he went on with his eyes closed: "Doc was in their way—and besides, Rose wanted the boat for himself."

Kells poured more whiskey into the glass. He said: "The *Joanna* came out tonight; how did they get the load?"

Kastner said: "She came out *last* night, an' they worked all night transferring cargo from a couple schooners—twelve hundred cases. The play was to run it in, three cases to a launch, each trip. They've got a swell federal connection at the wharf—the point was to get it by the cutters."

Kastner coughed again. "That's about all."

Fay went back to the desk, sat down. Kells held the glass of whiskey toward Kastner but Kastner shook his head. Kells drank a little of it.

Kastner went on listlessly: "Eddie an' me went to Perry's an' I busted in and waited for you. Doc was scared. That's the reason he'd wanted to see you: he had some kind of an in on what Rose was going to do an' wanted help. He was scared pea green."

Kells grinned at Fay.

Kastner twisted on the couch. Suddenly he spoke very rapidly, as if he wanted to say a great many things all at once: "Eddie waited down on the street to give me a buzz on the downstairs bell when you started up. Rose had called Reilly an' he was all set with three men to make the pinch—two in front an' one in the alley."

Kells asked: "How come you sapped Dave?"

"He was putting on an act for the girl so she wouldn't think he was in on it. He got too realistic."

Kells looked at Fay, spoke to Kastner: "I thought Reilly was Lee Fenner's man."

"He *was*. He was Fenner's best spot in the Police Department until Rose started selling him big ideas." Kastner's little face was growing very white.

Kells said: "There'll be a doctor here in a minute—I sent the launch ashore for one." Then he walked to a port and looked out at the paling sky. He spoke without turning: "Reilly's the Lou that Rose and O'Donnell were waiting for at the hotel. . . ."

"And he's the Lou they were waiting for on the boat—so they could let you have it resisting arrest—make it legal."

Kells went over to the desk. Fay was abstractedly playing with a small penknife; the woman still sat with her face between her hands.

Kells turned his head toward Kastner, asked very casually: "Who popped you?"

Kastner smiled a little. He said: "I don't remember."

The woman laughed. She put her hands on the table and threw her head back and laughed very loudly. Kastner looked at her and there was something inexpressibly cold and savage in his eyes.

Kells bent over the desk and took up a pen and wrote a few words on a piece of paper. He took the paper and the pen over to Kastner, said: "It'll make things a lot simpler if you sign this."

The little man glanced at the paper and his eyes were suddenly dull, empty. He said: "Nuts." He grinned at Kells, and then his face tightened and he died.

* * * * *

Kells and Fay sat at a table in Fay's apartment in Long Beach. The woman, Granquist, was asleep in a big chair. It was about eight-thirty, and outside it was gray and hot.

Kells said: "That's the way it'll have to be. None of us is worth a nickel as a witness."

Fay sipped his coffee and sat still for a little while; then he got up and went to the telephone and called Long Distance. He asked for a number in Los Angeles, waited a while, said: "Hello. This is Grant Fay. I want to talk to Fenner. . . ." There was a pause and then he said: "Wake him up."

28

He waited a little while and then he said: "Hello, Lee. . . . There's a friend of mine here with an idea . . ."

Fay gestured and Kells got up and went to the phone. He said: "This is Kells. . . . Reilly's double-crossing you. He and Jack Rose aim to take over the town. They're importing a lot of boys from the East, and you're on the wrong side of their list. . . ."

There was a long silence during which Kells held the receiver to his ear and grinned at Fay. Then he said: "My idea is that you reach Ruth Perry right away. She's *incommunicado* but you can beat that. Tell her there isn't any use trying to protect Dave any longer for Haardt's murder. Tell her that I said so. . . . Then see that she gets bail. When Dave finds out she's confessed, he'll have a lot of things to tell you. . . . Sure—he's guilty as hell."

Kells hung up and went back to the table. He said: "That oughta be that." He sat down and poured himself another cup of coffee and inclined his head toward Granquist.

Fay said: "She came out to the boat last night and said she'd been here a week or so from Detroit. She says she's got a million dollars' worth of information that she wants to peddle for five grand. She says it'll crack the administration wide open and that we can call our own shots next election."

Kells laughed quietly.

Fay went on expressionlessly: "I told her I wasn't in politics and wasn't in the market for her stuff, but she thought I was kidding her. She soaked up a couple bottles of Scotch and finally got down to twenty-five hundred. A few more slugs and she'd probably sell for a dollar ninety-eight. She said she needs new shoes."

Fay's Negro houseboy came in from the kitchen and cleared away the breakfast things.

Kells stood up. He said: "I'm going to take a nap while the wheels of justice make a couple turns." He went to the bedroom door, turned and spoke to the boy: "Call me in two hours." He went into the bedroom.

* * * * *

When the houseboy woke Kells, Fay had gone. Kells asked the boy to make some more coffee, shook Granquist awake.

"How about some Java?"

She said: "Sure."

They sat at the table and drank a great deal of coffee. Kells sent the boy out for a paper. RUTH PERRY CONFESSES HUSBAND SHOT HAARDT was spread across the front page.

Kells said: "Ain't nature wonderful!" He got up and put on a suit-coat Fay had given him. "I'm going to town."

Granquist said: "Me too. Can I ride with you?"

They went down and got into a cab and went to the parking station near the P & O wharf where Kells had left Cullen's car.

It was very hot, driving into Los Angeles. Kells took off his coat and drove in his shirtsleeves. His face was battered and Fay's shoes hurt his feet and he wanted very much to get into a bathtub and then get into bed.

He said: "Did you come out with Kastner and O'Donnell?"

Granquist looked at him out of the corners of her eyes, smiled sleepily. She said: "Uh huh."

"You O'Donnell's girl?"

"My God, no! I just came along for the ride." She slid down into the corner of the seat and closed her eyes.

Kells said: "Do you think O'Donnell shot Kastner?"

He looked at her. She nodded with her eyes closed.

He parked the car off Eighth Street and they went into a side entrance of the hotel, up the service stairway to Kells' room. He said: "I'll have to go downtown for questioning this afternoon—if they don't pick me up before. I want to have four or five hot baths and a little shut-eye first."

He went into the bathroom and turned on the water, took off his clothes and put on a long dark-green robe. When he came out, Granquist had curled up on the divan, was asleep. She had taken off her hat—awry honey-colored hair curved over her face and throat.

The telephone buzzed while Kells was in the tub. It buzzed again after he'd got out. He answered it, stared vacantly out the window and said: "All right—put her on." Then he said: "Hello, Ruth. . . . Swell. . . . No, I've got to go out right away and I won't be back until tonight. I'll try to give you a ring then. . . . Sure. . . . Okay, baby—'bye."

Granquist stirred in sleep, threw one arm above her

head, sighed. Her eyelids fluttered. Kells stood there for a while looking at her.

*   *   *   *   *

At one-thirty, Kells got out of a cab and went into the Sixth Street entrance of the Hayward Hotel. In the elevator he said: "Four." Around two turns, down a short corridor, he knocked at a heavy old-fashioned door.

A voice yelled: "Come in."

There were three men in the small room. One sat at a typewriter near the window. He had a leathery good-natured face and he spoke evenly into the telephone beside him: "Sure. . . . Sure. . . ."

The other two were playing cooncan on a suit-box balanced on their laps. One of them put down his hand, put the suit-box carefully on the floor, stood up.

Kells said: "Fenner."

The man at the telephone put one hand over the mouth-piece, turned his head to call through an open door behind him: "A gent to see you, Lee."

The man who had stood up walked to the door and nodded at someone in the next room and turned to Kells. "In here."

Kells went past him into the room and closed the door behind him.

That room was larger. Fenner, a slight, silver-haired man of about fifty, was lying on a bed in his trousers and under-shirt. There was an electric light on the wall behind the bed. Fenner put down the paper he had been reading and swung up to sit facing Kells. He said, "Sit down," and picked up his shoes and put them on. Then he went over and raised the blind on one of the windows that looked out on Spring Street. He said: "Well, Kells—is it hot enough for you?"

Kells nodded, said sarcastically: "You're harder to see than De Mille. I called your hotel and they made me get a Congressional Okay and make out a couple dozen affidavits before they gave me this number." He jerked his head toward the little room through which he had entered. "What's it all about?"

Fenner sat down in a big chair and smiled sleepily. He took a crumpled package of Home Runs out of his pocket,

31

extracted a cigaret and lighted it. "About a year ago," he said, "a man named Dickinson—a newspaperman—came out here with a bright idea and a little capital, and started a scandal sheet called the *Coaster*."

Fenner inhaled his cigaret deeply, blew a soft gray cone of smoke toward the ceiling. "He ran it into the ground on the blackmail side and got into a couple libel jams. . . ."

Kells said: "I remember."

Fenner went on: "I got postponements on the libel cases and I got the injunction raised. Now it's the *Coast Guardian; A Political Weekly For Thinking People*. Dickinson is still the editor and publisher, and"—he smiled thinly—"I'm the silent partner. The first number comes out next week—no sale, we give it away."

Kells said: "The city campaign ought to start rolling along about next week. . . ."

Fenner slapped his knee in mock surprise. "By George! That's a coincidence." He sat grinning contentedly at Kells. Then his face hardened a little and a faint, fanatical twinkle came into his eyes. He spoke, and it was as if he had said the same thing many times before: "I'm a *working* boss, Mister Kells. I gave this city the squarest deal it ever had. They beat my men at the polls last time but by God they didn't beat me—and next election day I'm going to take the city back."

Kells said: "I doubt it." He smiled a little to take the edge off his words, went on: "What did you get from Perry?"

"Nothing." Fenner yawned. "I got to his wife right after you called and gave her your message and arranged for her bail. She's witness number one for the State. It took me a little longer to beat the *incommunicado* on Perry, and when I saw him and told him she had confessed, he closed up like a clam."

Kells took off his hat and rubbed his scalp violently with his fingers. "It must have taken a lot of pressure to make a yellow bastard like him pipe down."

Fenner said: "Who killed Haardt?"

"Perry'll do for a while, won't he?" Kells put on his hat.

"Are you sure you're in the clear?"

"Yes." Kells stood up. "You've got enough to work on. Lieutenant Reilly, who was your best in the force, is in a play with Jack Rose to take over the town and open it up over your head. Dave Perry was in on it. They want it all—and they figure that you and I and a few more of the boys are in their way."

He walked over to the window and looked down at the swarming traffic on Spring Street. "Doc Haardt was in their way—figure it out for yourself."

Fenner said: "You act like you know what you're talking about."

"I do."

Fenner went on musingly: "One of the advantages of a reform administration is that you can blame it for everything. Maybe opening up the town for a few weeks isn't such a bad idea."

"But it's nice to know about it when you're supposed to be the boss. . . ." Kells smiled. "And it won't be so hot when it gets so wide open that a few of Reilly and Rose's imports from the East come up here and shove a machine gun down your throat."

Fenner said: "No."

"Me—I'm going to scram," Kells went on. "I came out here to play, and by God if I can't play here I'll go back to Broadway. My fighting days are over."

Fenner stared quizzically at Kells' bruised, battered face, smiled. "You'd better stick around," he said—"I like you."

"That's fine." Kells went to a table and poured himself a glass of water from a big decanter. "No—I'm going down to the station and see if they want to ask me any questions, and then I'm going home and pack. I've got reservations on the *Chief:* six o'clock."

Fenner stood up. "That's too bad," he said. "I have a hunch that you and I would be a big help to one another."

He held out his hand. Kells shook it, turned and went to the door. Then he turned again, slowly. "One other thing," he said. "There's a gal out here—name's Granquist—came out with a couple of Rose's boys; claims to have a million dollars' worth of lowdown on the administration. I can't use it. Maybe you can get together."

Fenner said: "Fine. How much does she want?"

Kells hesitated a bare moment. "Fifteen grand."

Fenner whistled. "It must be good," he said. "Send her

33

out to my hotel. Send her out tonight—I'll throw a party for her."

"She'll go for that. A lush." Kells smiled and went out the door and closed it behind him.

* * * * *

He went into the Police Station, into the Reporters' Room to the right of the entrance. Shep Beery looked up over his paper and said: "My God! What happened to your face?"

They were alone in the room. Kells looked with interest at the smudged pencil drawings on the walls, sat down. "I got it caught in a revolving door," he said. "Does anyone around here want to talk to me?"

"I do, for one." Beery put the paper down and leaned across the desk. He was a stoop-shouldered gangling man with a sharp sad face, a shock of colorless hair. "What's the inside on all this, Gerry?"

"All what?"

Beery spread the paper, pointed to headlines: PERRY INDICTED FOR HAARDT MURDER; WIFE CONFESSES. Beery's finger moved across the page: GAMBLING BARGE BURNS; 200 NARROWLY ESCAPE DEATH WHEN *JOANNA D* SINKS.

Kells laughed. "Probably just newspaper stories."

"No fooling, Gerry, give me a lead." Beery was intensely serious.

Kells asked: "You or your sheet?"

"That's up to you."

Kells trailed a long white finger over his discolored right eye. "If you read your paper a little more carefully," he said, "you'll find where an unidentified man was found dead near a wharf at San Pedro." He put his elbows on the desk, leaned close to Beery. "That's Nemo Kastner of Kansas City: He shot Doc Haardt on Jack Rose's order and helped frame it for me. He was shot by O'Donnell, his running mate, when they had an argument over the cut for Haardt's kill. He set fire to the ship. . . ."

". . . And swam four miles with a lungful of lead." Beery had been thumbing through the papers; pointed to the item.

"Uh huh."

"Who shot O'Donnell?"

Kells said: "You're too god-damned curious. Maybe it was Rose. Is he going to live?"

"Sure."

"That's swell." Kells took a deep breath.

"Now that's for *you*," he said. "Perry'll have to take the fall for Doc's murder for the time being; he was in on it plenty, anyway. Kastner's dead and I couldn't prove any of it without getting myself jammed up again. If anything happens to me you can use your own judgment, but until something happens that is all under your hat. Right?"

Beery nodded.

Kells stood up, said: "Now let's go upstairs and see if the captain can think of any hard ones."

They went out of the room into the corridor, upstairs.

Captain Larson was a huge watery-eyed Swede with a bulbous, thread-veined nose.

Beery said: "This is Kells. . . . He thought you might want to talk to him."

The captain shook his head slowly. He looked out the window and took a great square of linen out of his pocket and blew his nose. "No—I don't think so," he said slowly. "Cullen and the cab driver say you was at Cullen's house yesterday afternoon when Haardt was shot."

He looked up at Kells and his big mouth slit across his face to show yellow uneven teeth. "Was you?"

Kells smiled faintly, nodded.

"That's good enough for me." The captain blew his nose again noisily, folded the handkerchief carefully and put it in his pocket. "Perry's the only one who says you killed Doc. Lieutenant Reilly thinks you did but we can't run this department on thinks. . . . I think Perry's guilty as hell."

They all nodded sagely.

Kells said: "So long, Captain." He and Beery started out of the room.

The captain spoke again as Kells went through the door: "Where was you last night?"

Kells turned. "I was drunk. I don't remember." His eyes glittered with amusement.

The big man looked at him and his face wrinkled slowly to a grin. "Me too," he said. He slapped his thigh and laughed—a terrific crashing guffaw. His laughter followed

Kells and Beery down the stairs, through the corridor, echoing and re-echoing.

Beery said: "See you in church."

Kells went out into the sunlight, walked down First to Broadway, up Broadway to his bank.

The teller told him he had a balance of five thousand, one hundred and thirty dollars. He asked that the account be transferred to a New York bank, then changed his mind.

"I'll take it in cash."

The teller gave him five thousand-dollar notes, a hundred, a twenty and a ten-dollar bill. Kells took the sheaf of twenty-four new hundred-dollar bills out of his pocket and exchanged twenty of them for two more thousand-dollar notes. He folded the seven thousand-dollar notes and put them in a black pin-seal cardcase, put the case in his inside breast pocket. He put the five hundreds and the smaller bills in his trouser pocket and went out and got into a cab.

He said "Ambassador" and looked at his watch. It was two-forty; he had three hours and twenty minutes to get home and pack and make the *Chief*.

* * * * *

"Gerry." Granquist called to him as he crossed the lobby.

He waited until she had crossed to him, smiled ingenuously. "Gerry in the hay, baby," he said gently. "Mister Kells in public."

She laughed softly—a metallic softness.

Kells asked: "Did you get my note?"

"Uh huh." She spoke rapidly, huskily. "I woke up right after you left, I guess. Your phone's been raising bloody hell. I'm going home and get some sleep. . . ."

She held out a closed, black-gloved hand; Kells took his key.

He said: "Come on back upstairs—I've found a swell spot for your stuff."

"Oh—yeah?" Her face brightened.

They went to the elevator, up to Kells' room. Granquist sat in a steel-gray leather chair with her back to the windows, and Kells walked up and down.

"Lee Fenner has been the boss of this town for about six years," he said. "The reform element moved in last election, but Fenner's kept things pretty well under control—he has beautiful connections all the way to Washington. . . ."

He paused while Granquist took out tobacco and papers, started to roll a cigaret.

"You wanted to sell your stuff to Fay for five grand," he went on. "If it's as good as you think it is we can get fifteen from Fenner. . . . That's ten for you and five for me"—he smiled a little—"as your agent. . . ."

Granquist said: "I was drunk when I talked to Fay. Fifteen's chicken-feed. If you want to help me handle this the way it should be handled we can get fifty."

"You have big ideas, baby. Let's keep this practical."

Granquist lighted her cigaret, said: "How would you like to buy me a drink?"

Kells went into the dressing room and took two bottles of whiskey out of a drawer. He tore off the tissue paper wrappings and went back into the room and put them on a table.

"One for you and one for me." He took a cork-screw out of his pocket.

The phone buzzed.

Kells went to the phone, and Granquist got up and took off her gloves and began opening the bottles.

Kells said: "Hello. . . . Yes—fine, Stella. . . . Who? . . . Not Kuhn, Stella—maybe it's Cullen. . . . Yeah. . . . Put him on. . . ." He waited a moment, said: "Hello, Willie . . . Sure. . . ." He laughed quietly. "No, your car's all right. I'll send one of the boys in the garage out with it, or bring it out myself if I have time. . . . I'm taking a powder. . . . The *Chief:* six o'clock. . . . Uh huh, they're too tough out here for me. I'm going back to Times Square where it's quiet. . . . Okay, Willie. Thanks, luck—all that . . . G'bye."

He hung up, went to the table and picked up one of the opened bottles. He said: "Do you want a glass or a funnel?"

Granquist took the other bottle and sat down, jerked her head toward the phone. "Was that on the square—you're going?"

"Certainly."

"You're a sap." She tilted the bottle to her mouth, gurgled.

Kells went to a little table against one wall, took two glasses from a tray and went back and put them on the

37

center table. He poured one of them half full. "No, darling—I'm a very bright fella." He drank. "I'm going to get myself a lot of air while I can. The combination's too strong. I'm not ambitious. . . ."

"You're a sap."

Kells went to a closet and took out two traveling bags, a large suitcase. He took the drawers out of a small wardrobe trunk, put them on chairs.

"You'd run out on a chance to split fifty grand?" She was elaborately incredulous.

Kells started taking things out of the closets, putting them in the trunk. "Your information is worth more to Fenner than anyone else," he said. "If it's worth that much he'll probably pay it. You can send me mine. . . ."

"No, goddamn it! You stay here and help me swing this or you don't get a nickel."

Kells stopped packing, turned wide eyes toward Granquist. "Listen, baby," he said slowly, "I've *got* a nickel. I'm getting along swell legitimately. You take your bottle and your extortion racket, and screw. . . ."

Granquist laughed. She got up and went to Kells and put her arms around his body. She didn't say anything, just looked at him and laughed.

The wide, wild look went out of his eyes slowly. He smiled. He said: "What makes you think it's worth that much?"

Then he put her arms away gently and went to the table and poured two drinks.

3

At about six-forty Kells dropped Granquist at her apartment house on the corner of Wilcox and Yucca.

"Meet you in an hour at the Derby."

She said: "Oke—adiós."

Kells drove up Wilcox to Cahuenga, up Cahuenga to Iris, turned up the short curving slope to Cullen's house. The garage doors were open, he drove the car in and then went up and rang the bell. No one answered. He went back down and closed the garage doors and walked down to Cahuenga, down Cahuenga to Franklin.

He stood on the corner a little while and then went into a delicatessen and called a Hempstead number. The line was busy, he waited a few minutes, called again, said: "Hello, Ruth . . . Swell . . . Listen: I'm going to be very busy tonight—I've got about a half-hour. . . . You come out and walk up to Las Palmas, and if you're sure you're not tailed come up Las Palmas to Franklin. . . . If you're not absolutely sure take a walk or something. . . . I'll give you a ring late. . . . Yeah. . . ."

He went out and walked over Franklin to Las Palmas. He walked back and forth between Las Palmas and Highland for ten minutes and then walked down the west side of Las Palmas to Hollywood Boulevard. He didn't see anything of Ruth Perry.

He went on down Las Palmas to Sunset, east to Vine and up Vine to the Brown Derby.

Granquist was in a booth, far back, on the left.

She said: "I ordered oysters."

Kells sat down. "That's fine." He nodded to an acquaintance at a nearby table.

"A couple minutes after you left me," she said, "a guy came into my place and asked the girl at the desk who I was. She said 'Who wants to know?' and he said he had seen me come in and thought I was an old friend of his . . ."

"And . . ."

"And I haven't got any old friends."

"What'd he look like?" Kells was reading the menu.

"The girl isn't very bright. All she could remember was that he had on a gray suit and a gray cap."

Kells said: "That's a pipe—it was one of the Barrymores."

"No." Granquist shook her head very seriously. "It might've been a copper who tailed us from your hotel, or it might've been one of—"

Kells interrupted her suddenly: "Did you leave the stuff in your apartment?"

"Certainly not."

Kells said: "Anyway—we've got to do whatever's to be done with it tonight. I'm getting the noon train tomorrow."

"*We're* getting the noon train."

Kells smiled, looked at her a little while. He said: "When you can watch a lady eat oysters and still think she's swell— that's love."

He ordered the rest of the dinner.

Granquist carried a smart black bag. She opened it and took out a big silver flask, poured drinks under the table. The dinner was very good.

After a while, Granquist said with sudden and exaggerated seriousness: "I haven't told you the story of my life!"

Kells was drinking his coffee, watching the door. He turned to her slowly, said slowly: "No—but I've heard one."

"All right. *You* tell *me*."

"I was born of rich but honest parents. . . ."

"You can skip that."

He grinned at her. "I came back from France," he said, "with a set of medals, a beautiful case of shell shock and a morphine habit you could hang your hat on."

He gestured with his hands. "All gone."

"Even the medals?"

He nodded. "The State kept them as souvenirs of my first trial."

Granquist poured two drinks.

"I happened to be too close to a couple of front-page kills," Kells went on. "There was a lot of dumb sleuthing and a lot of dumb talk. It got so, finally, when the New York police couldn't figure a shooting any other way, I was it."

Granquist was silent, smiling.

"They got tired trying to hang them on me after the first three but the whisper went on. It got to be known as the *Kells Inside*. . . ."

"And at heart you're just a big, sympathetic boy who wouldn't hurt a fly."

"Uh, huh." He nodded his head slowly, emphatically. His face was expressionless.

"Me—I'm Napoleon." Granquist took a powder puff out of the bag and rubbed it over her nose.

Kells beckoned a waiter, paid the check. "And beyond the Alps lies Italy. Let's go." It was raining a little.

Kells held Granquist close to him. "The Knickerbocker is just around the corner on Ivar," he said—"but I'm going to put you in a cab and I want you to go down to Western Avenue and get out and walk until you're sure you're not being followed. Then get another cab and come to the Knickerbocker—I'll be in ten-sixteen."

The doorman held a big umbrella for them and they walked across the wet sidewalk and Granquist got into a cab. Kells stood in the thin rain until the cab had turned the corner down Hollywood Boulevard, then he went back into the restaurant.

Ruth Perry was sitting in the corner booth behind the cashier's desk. She didn't say anything. Kells sat down. There was a newspaper on the table and he turned it around, glanced at the headlines, said: "What do you think about the European situation?"

"Who was that?" Ruth Perry inclined her head slightly toward the door.

Kells put his elbows on the table and rubbed his eyes with his fingers. "None of your business, darling." He looked up at her and smiled. "Now keep your pants on. I stand to make a ten- or fifteen-thousand-dollar lick tonight, and *that* one"—he gestured with his head toward the door—"is a very important part of the play."

Ruth Perry leaned back and looked at the ceiling and laughed a little bit. Presently she said: "What are you going a do about Dave?"

"What do you want me to do?"

"I'm not going to go on the stand and lay myself open to a perjury rap."

Kells shook his head. "You won't have to, baby. The trial won't come up for a month or so and we can spring Dave before that"—he smiled with his mouth—"if you want to."

They were silent for a little while.

Then Kells said: "I've got to go now—call you around twelve."

He got up and went out into the rain. He walked up to the corner of Vine and Hollywood Boulevard and went into the drugstore and bought some aspirin, took two five-grain tablets and then went out and crossed the Boulevard and walked up Vine Street about a hundred yards. Then he crossed the street and walked back down to the parking station next to the Post Office. He stood on the sidewalk watching people across the street for a little while, then went swiftly back through the parking station and down the ramp to the garage under the Knickerbocker Hotel.

* * * * *

He got out of the elevator on the tenth floor and knocked at the door of ten-sixteen. Fenner opened the door.

Fenner said: "Well, Mister Kells—you didn't catch your train." He smiled and bowed Kells in.

They sat in the big living room and Fenner poured drinks. He poured three drinks and leaned back and asked: "Where's the little lady?"

"She'll be up in a few minutes."

Someone came out of the bathroom and through the bedroom. Fenner got up and introduced the dark medium-sized man that came in. "This is Bob Jeffers—God's gift to Womanhood . . . Mister Kells."

Kells stood up and shook hands with Jeffers. He was a motion-picture star who had had a brief and spectacular career; had been on the way out for nearly a year. He was drunk. He said: "It is a great pleasure to meet a real gunman, Mister Kells."

Kells glanced at Fenner and Fenner shook his head slightly, smiled apologetically. Kells sat down and sipped his whiskey.

Jeffers said: "I'm going up and get Lola." He took up his glass and went unsteadily out of the room, through the hallway, out the outer door.

"You mustn't mind Jeffers."

Kells said: "Sure." Then he leaned back in his chair and stared vacantly at Fenner. "Have you got twenty-five grand in cash?"

Fenner looked at him very intently. Then he smiled slowly and shook his head. "No," he said. "Why?"

"Can you get it—tonight?"

"Well—possibly. I—"

Kells interrupted, spoke rapidly. "I've talked to the lady. She's got enough on Bellmann to run him out of politics— out of the state, by God! You're getting first crack at it because I have a hunch he isn't sitting so pretty financially. It's the keys to the city for you—it's in black and white—an' it's a bargain."

"You seem to have a more than casual interest in this . . ."

Kells nodded. "Uh, huh," he said, smiled. "I'm the fiscal agent."

Fenner stood up and walked up and down the room, his hands clasped behind him, a lecture-platform expression on his face.

"You forget, Kells, that the Common People—the voters—are not fully informed of Mister Bellmann's connections, his power in the present administration."

"That's what your *Coast Guardian*'s for."

Fenner stopped in front of Kells. "Just what form does this, uh—incriminating information take?"

Kells shook his head, slowly. "You'll have to take my word for that," he said. He leaned forward and put his empty glass on the table.

The doorbell rang. Fenner went out into the hall, followed Granquist back into the room. Kells got up and introduced her to Fenner, and Fenner took her coat into the bedroom and then came back and poured drinks for all of them.

"Mister Kells has raised the ante to twenty-five thousand," he said. He smiled boyishly at Granquist.

She took her drink and sat down. She raised the glass to her mouth. "Hey, hey."

They all drank.

Granquist took a sack of Durham, papers out of her bag, rolled a cigaret.

Fenner said: "Of course I can't enter into a proposition involving so much money without knowing definitely what I'm getting."

"You put twenty-five thousand dollars in cash on the line and you get enough to put the election on ice." Kells got up and went over to one of the windows. He turned, went on very earnestly: "And it's a hell of a long ways from that now."

Fenner pursed his lips, smiled a little. "Well—now . . ."

"And it's got to be done *tonight*."

Granquist got up and put her empty glass on the table.

Fenner said: "Help yourself, help yourself."

She filled the two glasses on the table with whiskey and

43

ice and White Rock. She said: "Do you let strangers use your bathroom?"

Fenner took her through the hallway to the bedroom and turned on the light in the bath, came back and sat down and picked up the telephone, asked for a Mister Dillon. When the connection was made, he said: "I want you to bring up the yellow sealed envelope that's in the safe. . . . Yes, please—and bring it yourself." He hung up and turned to Kells. "All right," he said, "I'll play."

Kells sat down and crossed his legs. He studied the glistening toe of his left shoe, said: "It's going to sound like a fairy tale," looked up at Fenner. "Bellmann's a very smart guy. If he wasn't he wouldn't be where he is."

Fenner nodded impatiently.

Kells said: "The smarter they are, the sappier the frame they'll go for. Bellmann spent weekend before last at Jack Rose's cabin at Big Bear." He leaned forward and took his glass from the table. "Rose has been trying to get a feeler to him for a long time, has tried to reach him through his own friends. A few weeks ago Rose took a big place on the lake not far from Bellmann's, invited Hugg and Mac Almon—Mac is very close to Bellmann—up for the fishing, or what have you? They all dropped in on Bellmann in a spirit of neighborliness, and he decided he'd been wrong about Rose all these years. Next day he returned the call. When Hugg and Mac came to the city they left Rose and Bellmann like that"—he held up two slim fingers pressed close together.

Granquist came in, sat down. Kells turned his head in her direction. Without letting his eyes focus directly on her, he said: "That's where baby comes in."

Fenner lighted a cigaret, coughed out smoke.

"She came out with friends of Rose from K C," Kells went on. "Bellmann met her at Rose's and took her big. That was Rose's cue. He threw a party—one of those intimate, quiet little affairs—Rose and a showgirl, Bellmann and"—he smiled faintly at Granquist—"this one. They all got stiff—I don't mean drunk, I mean stiff. And what do you suppose happened?"

He paused, grinned happily at Fenner. "Miss Granquist had her little camera along, took a lot of snapshots." He turned his grin toward Granquist. "Miss Dipso Granquist stayed sober enough to snap her little camera."

Fenner got up and took Granquist's empty glass, filled it. He looked very serious.

Kells went on: "Of course it all came back to Rose in the morning. He asked about the pictures and she gave him a couple of rolls of film she'd stuck in the camera during the night, clicked with the lens shut, blanks. She discovered that the lens wasn't open when she gave them to him, they had one of those morning-after laughs about it. Bellmann had a dark green hangover; he didn't even remember about the pictures until a day or so later and then he wrote Miss Granquist a couple of hot letters with casual postscripts: 'How did the snapshots turn out, darling?' cracks like that."

Kells got up, stretched. "You see, it gets better as it goes along."

"What are the pictures like?" Fenner was standing near Granquist, his little pointed chin thrust toward Kells.

"Don't be silly. They're right out of the pocket of one of those frogs that work along the Rue de Rivoli." Kells ran his fingers through his hair. "That's not the point though. It's not what they are, it's who they're of: Mister John R. Bellmann, the big boss of the reform administration, the Woman's Club politician—at the house and in the intimate company of Jack Rose, gambler, Crown Prince of the Western Underworld and a couple of, well—questionable ladies."

"And exactly what am I buying?"

"The negatives and one set of prints. My word that you're getting all the negatives and that there are no other prints. The letters—and certain information as to what Bellmann and Rose talked about before they went under. . . ."

The doorbell rang.

Fenner said: "That'll be Dillon." He went out into the hallway and came back with a sandy-haired, spectacled man. Both of them were holding their hands above their shoulders in the conventional gesture of surprise. Two men whom Kells had never seen before came in behind them. One, the most striking, was rather fat and his small head

45

stack out of a stiff collar, his tie was knotted to stick straight out, stiffly from the opening in his collar. He held a short blunt revolver in his hand.

* * * * *

The fat man said: "Go see if the tall one has got anything in his pockets."

The other man went to Kells. He was a gray-faced nondescript young man in a tightly belted raincoat. He went through Kells' pockets very carefully and when he had finished, said: "Sit down."

Dillon shifted his weight from one foot to the other and the fat man, who was almost directly behind him, raised the revolver and brought the muzzle down hard on the back of his head. Dillon grunted and his knees gave away and he slumped down softly to the floor.

The fat man giggled quietly, nervously. He said: "That's one down. Every little bit helps."

Kells sat down on the divan and leaned back and crossed his legs.

The fat man said: "Put your hands up, Skinny." Kells shook his head slightly.

The young man in the raincoat leaned forward and slapped Kells across the mouth. Kells looked up at him and his face was very sad, his eyes were sleepy. He said: "That's too bad."

Fenner turned his head, spoke over his shoulder to the fat man: "What do you want?"

"I don't want you. Go sit down in that chair by the window."

Fenner crossed the room, sat down.

The fat man said: "Reach back of you and pull the shades shut."

Granquist said sarcastically: "Now pull up a chair for yourself, Chub." She leaned forward toward the table. "Ain't you going to have a drink?"

Kells said: "Don't say 'ain't,' sweet."

The fat man sat down in the chair nearest the door. His elbows were on the arms of the chair and he held the revolver loosely on his lap, said: "I want a bunch of pictures that you tried to peddle to Bellmann, girlie."

"Don't call me girlie, you son of a bitch!"

Kells looked at Granquist, shook his head sadly. "That's something you forgot to tell me about," he said.

"I want all the pictures," the fat man repeated, "an' I want two letters—quick."

Granquist was staring at the fat man. She turned slowly to Kells. "That's a lie, Gerry. I didn't crack to Bellmann."

Fenner stood up. "I won't stand for this," he said. He thrust his hands in his pockets and took a step forward.

"Sit down." The fat man moved the revolver slightly until it focused on Fenner's stomach.

Fenner stood still.

Kells said: "Does the fella who sent you know that if anything happens to me the whole inside gets a swell spread in the morning papers?"

The fat man smiled.

"The inside on Haardt and the barge and Perry, and the Sunday-school picnic at Big Bear?" Kells went on.

Granquist was watching him intently.

"I made that arrangement this afternoon." Kells leaned sidewise slowly and put his empty glass on an end table.

The fat man looked at Fenner and Kells, and then he looked at Granquist, and at the bag tucked into the chair beside her. He said: "That's a dandy. Let's have a look at it, girlie."

Granquist stood up in one swift and precise movement. She moved to the window so swiftly that the fat man had only time to stand up and take one step toward her before she had moved the drape aside with her shoulder, crashed the bag through the window.

Glass tinkled on the sill.

Kells stood up in the same instant and brought his right fist up from the divan in a long arc to the side of the gray-faced young man's jaw. The young man spun half around and Kells swung his right fist again to the same place. The young man fell half on the divan, half on the floor.

The fat man moved toward Kells, stopped in the center of the floor.

Granquist yelled: "Smack him, Gerry. . . ."

Kells stood with his feet wide apart. He grinned at the fat man.

Fenner was standing near Granquist at the window. His

eyes were wide and he tried to say something but the words stuck in his throat.

The fat man backed toward the door. "I ain't got orders to shoot," he said, "but I sure will if you press me." He backed out into the semidarkness of the hallway and then the outer door slammed.

Granquist ran across the room, stopped a moment in the doorway, turned her head toward Kells. She said, "I'll get the bag," and she spoke so rapidly, so breathlessly, that the words were all run together into one word. She went into the darkness.

Kells turned to Fenner. "Give her a hand."

He bent over the young man, took a small automatic out of his raincoat pocket and handed it to Fenner. "Hurry up—I've got to telephone—I'll be right down."

Fenner took the automatic dazedly. He looked at the man on the floor and at Kells, and then he came suddenly to life. "It's in the court," he said excitedly. "I can get out there from the third floor."

"Maybe the bag was a stall. Don't let her get out of your sight." Kells sat down at the telephone.

Fenner hurried out of the room.

Kells waited until he heard the outer door slam, then got up and went to Dillon. He knelt and drew a long yellow envelope from Dillon's inside breast pocket. It was heavily sealed. He tore off the end and looked inside. Then, smiling blankly, he tucked it into his pocket.

He went to the broken window, raised it carefully and leaned out over the wet darkness of the court for a moment. He went into the kitchen and stood on the stove, looked through the high ventilating window across the narrow airshaft to the window of an adjoining apartment. Then he went into the bedroom and got his hat and Granquist's coat and went out of the apartment, across the corridor to the elevator.

On the way down, he spoke to the elevator boy: "Is it still raining?"

"Yes, sir. It looks like it was going to rain all night."

Kells said: "I wouldn't be surprised."

The night clerk came out of the telephone operator's compartment.

Kells leaned on the desk. "Your Mister Dillon is in ten-sixteen. He had an accident. There's another man in there whom Fenner will file charges against. Have the house dick hold him till Fenner gets back."

He started to go, paused, said over his shoulder: "Maybe you'll find another one trying to get in or out of the court. Probably not."

He went out and walked up Ivar to Yucca, west on Yucca the short block to Cahuenga. The rain had become a gentle mist for the moment; it was warm, and occasional thunder drummed over the hills to the north. He went into an apartment house on the corner and asked the night man if Mister Beery was in.

"He went out about ten minutes ago." The night man thought he might be in the drugstore across the street.

Beery was crouched over a cup of coffee at the soda fountain. Kells sat down beside him and ordered a glass of water, washed down two aspirin tablets. He said: "If you want to come along with me, you *might* get some more material for your memoirs."

Beery put a dime on the counter and they went out, over to Wilcox. They went into the Wilcox entrance of the Lido, upstairs to the fourth floor and around through a long corridor to number four-thirty-two.

Granquist opened the door. Her face was so drained of color that her mouth looked dark and bloody in contrast to her skin. Her mouth was slightly open and her eyes were wide, burning. She held her arms stiffly at her sides.

There was a man lying on his face, half in, half out of the bathroom. His arms were doubled up under his body.

Beery walked past Granquist, slowly across the room to a table. He turned his head slowly as he walked, kept his eyes on the man on the floor. He took off his hat and put it on the table.

Kells closed the door quietly and stood with his back against it.

Granquist stared at him without change of expression.

Beery glanced at them.

Kells smiled a little. He said: "This isn't what I meant, Shep—maybe it's better."

Beery went to the man on the floor, squatted and turned the head sidewise.

Granquist swallowed. She said: "Gerry, I didn't do it. I didn't do it."

Beery spoke softly, without looking up: "Bellmann."

* * * * *

Kells locked the door. He looked at the floor, then he went to the table and reached under it with his foot, kicked an automatic out into the light.

Granquist walked unsteadily to a chair, sat down and stared vacantly at Beery bending over the body. She said in a hollow, monotonous voice: "He was like that when I came in. I stopped downstairs and then I came up in the elevator and he was like that when I came in—just a minute ago."

Kells didn't look at her. He took out a handkerchief and picked up the automatic and held it to his nose. He held it carefully by the handkerchief and snapped the magazine out of the grip, said: "Two."

Beery stood up.

Kells laughed suddenly. He threw back his head and roared with laughter. He sat down and put the automatic on the table, wiped his eyes with the handkerchief.

"It's beautiful!" he said brokenly.

Granquist stared at Kells and then she leaned back in the chair and her eyes were very frightened. She said: "I didn't do it," over and over again.

Kells' laughter finally wore itself out. He wiped his eyes with the handkerchief and then he looked up at Beery. "Well," he said, "why the hell don't you get on the phone? You've got the scoop of the season."

He leaned back and smiled at the ceiling, improvised headlines: "Boss Bellmann Bumped Off By Beauty. Pillar of Church Meets Maker. Politician—let's see—Politician Plugged as Prowler by Light Lady." He stood up and crossed quickly to Beery, emphasized his words with a long white finger against Beery's chest. "Here's a pip! Reformer Foiled in Rape. Killer says: 'I shot to save my honor, the priceless inheritance of American womanhood.' "

Beery went to the telephone. He said: "We've been a Bellmann paper—I'll have to talk to the Old Man."

"You god-damned idiot! No paper can afford to soft-

50

pedal a thing like this. Can't you see that without an editorial O K?"

Beery nodded in a faraway way, dialed a number. He asked for a Mister Crane; when Crane had answered, said: "This is Beery. Bellmann has been shot by a jane, in her apartment, in Hollywood . . . Uh huh—very dead."

He grinned up at Kells, listened to an evident explosion at the other end of the line. "We'll have to give it everything, Mister Crane," he went on. "It's open and shut—there isn't any out. . . . O K. Switch me to Thompson—I'll give it to him."

Granquist got up and went unsteadily to the door. She put her hand on the knob and then seemed to remember that the door was locked. She looked at the key but didn't touch it. She turned and went into the dinette, took a nearly empty bottle out of the cupboard and came back and sat down.

Beery asked: "What's your name, sister?"

Granquist was trying to get the cork out of the bottle. She didn't say anything or look up.

Kells said: "Granquist." He looked at her for a moment, then went over to the window, turned his head slightly toward Beery: "Miss Granquist."

Beery said, "Hello, Tom," spoke into the telephone in a low even monotone.

Kells turned from the window, crossed slowly to Granquist. He sat down on the arm of her chair and took the bottle out of her hand and took out the cork. He got up and went into the dinette, poured the whiskey into a glass and brought it back to her, sat down again on the arm of the chair. "Don't take it so big, baby," he said very softly and quietly. "You've got a perfect case. The jury'll give you roses and a vote of thanks on the 'for honor' angle—and it's the swellest thing that could happen for Fenner's machine—it's the difference between Bellmann's administration and a brand-new one . . ."

"I didn't do it, Gerry." She looked up at him and her eyes were dull, hurt. "I didn't do it! I left the snaps and stuff in the office downstairs when I went out—the bag was a gag. . . ."

Kells said: "I knew they weren't in the bag—you left it

51

in the chair when you went into the bathroom."

She nodded. She wasn't listening to him. She had things to say. "I ran back here when I left Fenner's. I picked up the stuff at the office—had to wait till the manager got the combination to the safe out of his apartment. Then I came up here to wait for you."

She drank, put the glass on the floor. She turned, inclined her head toward Bellmann. "He was like that. He must have come here for the pictures—he'd been through my things. . . ."

Kells said: "Never mind, baby—it's a set up. . . ."

"I didn't do it!" She beat her fist on the arm of the chair. Her eyes were suddenly wild.

Kells stood up.

Beery finished his report, hung up the receiver. He said: "Now I better call the station."

"Wait a minute." Kells looked down at Granquist and his face was white, hard. "Listen!" he emphasized the word with one violent finger. "You be nice. You play this the way I say and you'll be out in a month—maybe I can even get you out on bail. . . ."

He turned abruptly and went to the door, turned the key. "Or"—he jerked his head toward the door, looked at the little watch on the inside of his wrist—"there's a Frisco bus out Cahuenga in about six minutes. You can make it—and ruin your case."

Outside, sultry thunder rumbled and rain whipped against the windows. Kells slid a note off the sheaf in his breast pocket, went over and handed it to her. It was a thousand dollar note.

She looked at it dully, slowly stood up. Then she stuffed the note into the pocket of her suit and went quickly to the chair where Kells had thrown her coat.

Kells said: "Give me the pictures."

Beery was staring open-mouthed at Kells. "Gerry, you can't do this," he said. "I told Tommy we had the girl—"

"She escaped."

Granquist put on her coat. She looked at Kells and her eyes were soft, wet. She went to him and took a heavy manila envelope out of her pocket, handed it to him. She stood a moment looking up at him and then she turned and went to the door, put her hand on the knob and turned it, then took her hand away from the knob and held it up to her face. She stood like that a little while and then she said, "All right," very low.

She said, "All right," again, very low and distinctly, and turned from the door and went back to the big chair and sat down.

*   *   *   *   *

About ten minutes later Beery got up and let Captain Hayes of the Hollywood Division in. There were two plain-clothes men and an assistant coroner with him.

The assistant coroner examined Bellmann's body, looked up in a little while: "Instantaneous—two wounds, probably thirty-two caliber—one touched the heart." He stood up. "Dead about twenty minutes."

Hayes picked up the gun from where Kells had replaced it under the table, examined it, wrapped it carefully.

Kells smiled at him. "Old school—along with silencers and dictaphones. Nowadays they wear gloves."

Hayes said: "What's your name?"

Beery said: "Oh, I'm sorry—I thought you knew each other. This is Gerry Kells . . . Captain Hayes."

"What were you doing here?" Hayes was a heavily built man with bright brown eyes. He spoke very rapidly.

"Shep and I came up to call on my girl friend here"— Kells indicated Granquist who was still sitting with her coat on, staring at them all in turn, expressionlessly. "We found it just the way you see it."

Hayes glanced at Beery, who nodded. Hayes spoke to Granquist. "Is that right, miss?"

She looked up at him blankly for a moment, then nodded slowly.

"That'll be about all, I guess." Hayes looked at Kells. "You still at the Ambassador?"

"You can always reach me through Shep."

Hayes said: "Come on, miss."

Granquist got up and went into the dressing room and packed a few things in a small traveling bag.

One of the plain-clothes men opened the door, let two ambulance men in. They put Bellmann's body on a stretcher and carried it out.

Kells leaned against the doorframe of the dressing room, watched Granquist. "I'll be down in the morning with an attorney," he said. "In the meantime, keep quiet."

She nodded vaguely and closed the bag, came out of the dressing-room. She said: "Let's go."

The manager of the apartment house was in the corridor with one of the Filipino bellboys, a reporter from the *Journal* and a guest. The manager was wringing his hands. "I can't understand it—no one heard the shots."

One of the plain-clothes men looked superiorly at the manager, said: "The thunder covered the shots."

They all went down the corridor except Beery and Kells and the manager. The manager went to the door, smiled weakly at Kells. "I'll close up Miss Granquist's apartment."

Kells said: "Never mind—I'll bring the key down."

The manager was doubtful.

Kells looked very stern, whispered: "Special investigator." He and Beery went back into the apartment.

Beery called his paper again with additional information: "Captain Hayes made the arrest. . . . And don't forget: the *Chronicle* is always first with the latest. . . ." He hung up, lighted a new cigaret from the butt of another. "From now on," he said, "I'm going to follow you around and phone in the story of my life, from day to day."

Kells asked: "Are they giving it an extra?"

"Sure. It's on the presses now—be on the streets in a little while."

"That's dandy."

Kells went into the kitchen, switched on the light. He looked out the kitchen window and then he went to a tall cupboard—the kind of cupboard where brooms are kept in a modern apartment—opened the door.

Fenner came out, blinking in the bright light. He said: "I would have had"—he swallowed—"would have had to come out in another minute. I nearly smothered."

"That's too bad."

Beery stood in the doorway. He said: "For the love of—"

Fenner went past Beery into the living room, sat down. He was breathing hard.

Kells strolled in behind him and sat down across the room, facing him.

Fenner took out a handkerchief and dabbed at his mouth and forehead. He said: "I followed her as you suggested— and when she went in through the lobby, I came up the side stair intending to meet her up here."

Kells smiled gently, nodded.

"I didn't want to be seen following her through the lobby, you know."

"No."

Beery was still standing in the kitchen doorway, staring bewilderedly at Fenner.

"I knocked but she hadn't come up yet," Fenner went on, "so I opened the door—it was unlocked—and came in."

Kells said: "The door was unlocked?"

Fenner nodded. "In a few minutes I heard her coming up the hall and she was talking to a man. I went into the kitchen, of course, and she and Bellmann came in. They were arguing about something. Bellmann went into the bathroom I think, and then I heard the two shots during one of the peals of thunder. I didn't know what to do—and then when I was about to come out and see what had happened, you knocked at the door."

Fenner paused, took a long breath. "I didn't know it was you, of course, so I hid in the cupboard."

Kells said: "Oh."

"I thought it would be better if I didn't get mixed up in a thing of this kind, in any way."

Kells said, "Oh," again. Then he looked up at Beery, said: "Sit down, Shep—I want to tell you a story."

Beery sat down near the door.

Kells stretched one long leg over the arm of his chair, made himself comfortable. "This afternoon I told Mister Fenner"—he inclined his head toward Fenner in one slow emphatic movement—"that I knew a gal who had some very hot political info that she wanted to sell."

Beery nodded almost imperceptibly.

"He was interested and asked me to send her to his hotel tonight. I had a talk with her, and the stuff sounded so good that I got interested too—took her to Fenner's myself."

Fenner was extremely uncomfortable. He looked at Kells and dabbed at his forehead; his lips were bent into a faint forced smile.

"We offered the information—information of great political value—to Mister Fenner at a very fair price," Kells went on. "He agreed to it and called the manager of his hotel and asked him to bring up an envelope containing a large amount in cash."

Kells turned his eyes slowly from Beery to Fenner. "When the manager came in a couple of benders came in with him. They'd been waiting in the next apartment, listening across the airshaft to find out what they had to heist—it was supposed to look like Rose's stick-up—or Bellmann's. . . ."

Fenner stood up.

Kells said: "But it was Mister Fenner's. Mister Fenner wanted to eat his cake and have crumbs in his bed, too."

Fenner took two steps forward. His eyes were flashing. He said: "That's a lie, sir—a tissue of falsehood!"

Kells spoke very softly, enunciating each word carefully, distinctly: "Sit down, you dirty son of a bitch."

Fenner straightened, glared at Kells. He half turned toward the door.

Kells got up and took three slow steps, then two swiftly, crashed his fist into Fenner's face. There was a sickening crackly noise and Fenner fell down very hard.

Kells jerked him up and pushed him back into the chair. Kells' face was worried, solicitous. He said very slow—almost whispered: "Sit still."

Then he went back to his chair and sat down, went on: "One of the hoys sapped the manager. They fanned me and made a pass for Granquist's handbag. She tossed it out the window; I smacked one of them and the other one went after the bag. Granquist faked going after the bag too and I sent Fenner after her, figuring that the stuff wasn't in the bag and that she'd come back here and that the three of us would get together here for another little talk."

Fenner was pressing himself back into the corner of the chair. He was holding his hands to his bloody face and moaning a little.

"When I sent Fenner after Granquist," Kells went on, "I gave him a gun—one of the boy's. He was so excited about getting to the bag, or keeping G in sight that he forgot to frisk the manager for his big dough. . . ."

Kells took the yellow envelope out of his pocket. "So I got it." He leaned forward, pressed the edges of the envelope and a little packet of cigar coupons fell out on the floor.

"Almost enough to get a package of razor blades."

Beery grinned.

Kells said: "Granquist headed over here, so Fenner knew that the bag had been a stall, followed her. When she came in past the office he ducked up the side way and, figuring that she had come right up, knocked at her door."

Beery said: "How did he know which apartment was hers?"

"He had us tailed from my hotel early this evening. His man got her number from the mail-boxes in the lobby, gave it to him before we got to his place tonight."

Beery nodded.

Kells said: "Am I boring you?"

"Yes. Bore me some more."

"Bellmann had come up here after some things he wanted—some very personal things that he couldn't trust anyone else to get. He probably paid his way into the apartment—I'll have to check up on that—and didn't find what he was looking for, and when Fenner knocked he thought it was either Granquist, who he wanted to talk to anyway, or whoever let him in."

Kells took a deep breath. "He opened the door, and . . ."

Kells paused, got up and went to Fenner, looked down at the little twisted man and smiled. "Mister Fenner knows a good thing when he sees it—he jockeyed Bellmann into a good spot and shot him through the heart."

Fenner mumbled something through his hands.

"He waited for a nice roll of off-stage thunder and murdered him."

Beery said: "That's certainly swell. And I haven't got any more job than a rabbit." He stood up, stared disconsolately at Kells. "My God! Bellmann killed by the boss of the opposition—the most perfect political break that could happen, for my paper—and I turn in an innocent girl, swing it exactly the other way politically. My God!"

Beery sat down and reached for the telephone.

Kells said: "Wait a minute."

Beery held up his right hand, the forefinger pointed,

brought it down emphatically towards Kells. "Nuts!"

Kells said: "Wait a minute, Shep." His voice was very gentle. His mouth was curved in a smile and his eyes were very hot and intent.

Beery sat still.

Fenner got up. Holding a darkening handkerchief to his face, he tottered toward the door.

Kells went past him to the door, locked it. He said: "Both you bastards pipe down and sit still till I finish."

He shoved Fenner back into the chair.

"As I was about to say: you were a little late, you heard Granquist outside the door, wiped off the rod—if you didn't, *I* did—put it under the table and ducked into the cupboard."

Beery said slowly: "What do you mean: *you* wiped it off?"

Kells didn't answer. He squatted in front of Fenner, said: "Listen, you—what do you think I put on that act for—ribbed Granquist into taking the fall? Because *she* can beat it." His elbows were on his knees. He pointed his finger forcibly at Fenner, sighted across it. "*You* couldn't. You couldn't get to first base. . . ."

Fenner's face was a bruised, fearful mask. He stared blankly at Kells.

"A few days ago—yesterday—all I wanted was to be let alone," Kells went on. "I wasn't. I was getting along fine—quietly—legitimately—and Rose and you and the rest of these —— —— gave me action."

He stood up. "All right—I'm beginning to like it." He walked once to the window, back, bent over Fenner. "I'm taking over your organization. Do you hear me? *I'm* going to run this town for a while—ride hell out of it."

He glanced at Beery, smiled. Then he turned again to Fenner, spoke quietly: "I was going East tomorrow. Now *you're* going. You're going to turn everything over to me and take a nice long trip—or they're going to break your goddamned neck with a rope."

Kells went to the small desk, sat down. He found a pen, scribbled on a piece of Lido stationery. "And just to make it 'legal, and in black and white,' as the big business men say—you're going to sign this—and Mister Beery is going to witness it."

Beery said: "You can't get away with a—"

"No?" Kells paused, glanced over his shoulder at Beery. "I'll get away with it big, young fella. And stop worrying about your job—you've got a swell job with me. How would you like to be chief of police?"

He went on writing, then stopped suddenly, turned to Fenner. "I've got a better idea," he said. "You'll stay here where I can hold a book on you. You stay here and in your same spot—only you can't go to the toilet without my okay." He got up and stood in the center of the room and jerked his head toward the desk. "There it is. Get down on it—quick."

Fenner said, "Certainly not," thickly.

Kells looked at the floor, said: "Call Hayes, Shep."

Beery reached for the telephone.

Fenner didn't look at him. He held his hands tightly over his face for a moment, mumbled, "My God!"—then he got up and went unsteadily to the desk, sat down. He stooped over the piece of paper, read it carefully.

Kells said: "If Granquist beats the case—and she will—and you don't talk out of turn, I'll tear it up in a month or so."

Fenner picked up the pen, shakily signed.

Kells looked at Beery, and Beery got up and went over and read the paper. He said: "This is a confession. Does it make me an accessory?"

Kells said: "It isn't dated."

Beery signed and folded the paper and handed it to Kells.

Kells glanced at it, turned to Fenner. "Now I want you to call your *Coast Guardian* man, Dickinson, and any other key men you can get in touch with, and tell them to be at your joint at the Knickerbocker in a half-hour."

Fenner went into the bathroom, washed his face. He came back in a little while and sat down at the telephone.

Kells held the folded paper out to Beery. "You're going downtown anyway, Shep," he said. "Stick this in the safe at your office—I'll be down in the morning and take it to the bank."

Beery said: "Do I look that simple? I've got a wife and family."

Kells put the folded paper in his own pocket.

59

"Anyway, I'm not going downtown. I'm coming along." Beery picked up his hat.

Kells nodded abstractedly, glanced at his watch; it was twenty-two minutes past ten. Outside, there was a long ragged buzz of faraway thunder and the telephone clicked as Fenner dialed a number.

4

Five men sat in Fenner's apartment at the Knickerbocker. Fenner sat at one end of the divan. Hanline, Fenner's secretary, sat beside him, then Abe Gowdy, Fenner's principal contact man with the liberal element. They hadn't been able to reach Dickinson.

Gowdy swung the vote of practically every gambler, grafter, bootlegger and so on in the county, except the few independents who tried to get along without protection. He was a bald, paunchy man with big white bulbs of flesh under his eyes, a loose pale mouth. He wore dark, quiet clothes; didn't drink.

Hanline was a curly-haired, thin-nosed Jew. He drank a great deal.

He and Beery and Kells all drank a great deal.

Kells got up and walked to one of the windows. He said: "Try him again."

Fenner reached wearily for the phone, asked for a Fitzroy number, listened a little while and hung up.

Kells turned, came back and stopped near Fenner, looked first at Gowdy, then Hanline.

"Gentlemen," he said. "Lee"—he indicated Fenner with a fond pat on the shoulder—"Lee and I have entered into a partnership." He paused, picked up a small glass full of whiskey and cracked ice, drank most of it.

"We all know," he went on, "that things haven't been so good the last three or four years—and we know that unless some very radical changes are made in the city government things won't get any better." Hanline nodded slightly.

"Lee and I have talked things over and decided to join forces." Kells put down the glass.

Gowdy said: "What do you mean: 'join forces,' Mister Kells?"

Kells cleared his throat, glanced at Beery. "You boys have the organization," he said. "You, Gowdy—and Frank Jensen, and O'Malley—and Lee here. My contribution is very important political information, which I'll handle in my own way and at my own time—and a lot of friends in the East who are going to be on their way out here tomorrow."

Hanline looked puzzled. Gowdy glanced expressionlessly at Fenner.

"Bellmann's dead," Kells went on—"and the circumstances of his murder can be of great advantage to us if they're handled in exactly the right way. But that, alone, isn't going to swing an election. We've got the personal following of all the administration to beat—and we've got Rose's outfit to beat. . . ."

Hanline asked: "Rose?"

Kells poured himself another drink. "Rose has built up a muscle organization of his own in the last few months—and a week or so ago he threw in with Bellmann."

Hanline and Gowdy glanced at one another, at Fenner.

Kells said: "There it is." He sat down.

Fenner got up and went into the bedroom. He came back presently, said: "It's a good proposition, Abe. Mister Kells wants to put the heat on Rose—"

Kells interrupted: "I want to reach Dickinson tonight and see if we can't get the first number of the *Guardian* on the streets by morning. There are certain angles on the Bellmann thing that the other papers won't touch."

Hanline said: "Maybe he's at Ansel's—but they won't answer the phone there after ten."

"Who's Ansel?"

Hanline started to answer but Gowdy interrupted him: "Did you know Rose was backing Ansel?" Gowdy was looking at Fenner.

Fenner shook his head, spoke to Kells: "Ansel runs a couple crap games down on Santa Monica Boulevard—Dickinson plays there quite a bit."

Kells said: "So Dickie is a gambler?"

Hanline laughed. "I'll bet he's made a hundred thousand dollars with the dirt racket in the last year," he said.

61

"And I'll bet he hasn't got a dollar and a quarter."

Kells smiled at Fenner. "You ought to take better care of your hired men," he said. Then he got up, finished his drink and put on his hat. "I'll go over and see if I can find him."

Beery said: "I'll come along."

Kells shook his head slightly.

Hanline stood up, stretched, said: "It's the second or third building on the south side of the street, west of Gardner—used to be a scene painter's warehouse or something like that—upstairs."

"Thanks." Kells asked Fenner: "Dickinson's the guy that was typewriting at the place downtown?"

Fenner nodded.

Hanline said: "If you don't mind, I'm going back downstairs and get some sleep. I was out pretty late last night."

"Sure." Kells glanced at Gowdy.

Kells and Hanline went out, down the elevator. Hanline got off at the fifth floor. Kells stopped at the desk, asked for the house detective. The clerk pointed out a heavy, dull-eyed man who sat reading a paper near the door. Kells went over to him, said: "You needn't hold the man Fenner was going to file charges against."

The house detective put down his paper. He said: "Hell, he was gone when I got upstairs. There wasn't nobody there but Mister Dillon."

Kells said: "Oh." He scratched the back of his head. "How's Dillon?"

"He'll be all right." Kells went out and got into a cab.

* * * * *

Ansel's turned out to be a dark, three-story business block set flush with the sidewalk. There were big For Rent signs in the plate-glass windows and there was a dark stairway at one side.

Kells told the cab driver to wait, went upstairs.

Someone opened a small window in a big heavily timbered door, surveyed him dispassionately.

Kells said: "I want to see Ansel."

"He ain't here."

"I'm a friend of Dickinson's—I want to see *him*."

The window closed and the door swung slowly open;

Kells went into a small room littered with newspapers and cigaret butts. The man who had looked at him through the window patted his pockets methodically, silently.

Another man, a very dark-skinned Italian or Greek, sat in a worn wicker chair tilted back against one wall.

He said: "Your friend Dickinson—he is very drunk."

Kells said, "So am I," and then the other man finished feeling his pockets, went to another heavy door, opened it.

Kells went into a very big room. It was dark except for two clots of bright light at the far end. He walked slowly back through the darkness, and the hum of voices grew louder, broke up into words: "Eight. . . . Point is eight, a three-way . . . Get your bets down, men. . . . Throws five—point is eight. . . . Throws eleven, a field point, men. . . . Throws four—another fielder. Get 'em in the field, boys. . . . Five . . . Seven, out. Next man. Who likes this lucky shooter? . . ."

Each of the two tables was lined two deep with men. One powerful green-shaded light hung over each table. The dice man's voice droned on: "Get down on him, boys. . . . Ten—the hard way. . . . Five. . . . Ten—the winner. . . . All right, boys, he's coming out. Chuck it in. . . ."

Kells saw Dickinson. He was standing at one end of one of the tables. He was swaying back and forth a little and his eyes were half closed; he held a thick sheaf of bills in his left hand.

"Seven—the winner. . . ."

Dickinson leaned forward and put his forefinger unsteadily down beside a stack of bills on the line. The change man reached over, counted it and put a like amount beside it.

"Drag fifty, Dick," he said. "Hundred-dollar limit."

Dickinson said thickly: "Bet it all."

The change man smiled patiently, picked up a fifty-dollar bill and tossed it on the table nearer Dickinson.

A small, pimpled old man at the end of the table caught the dice as they were thrown to him, put them into the black leather box, breathed into it devoutly, rolled.

Kells elbowed closer to the table.

"Eleven—the winner. . . ."

Dickinson stared disgustedly at the change man as a hundred dollars in tens and twenties was counted out, laid

63

down beside his line bet. The change man said: "Drag a C, Dick."

"Bet it!" Dickinson said angrily.

Kells looked at the change man. He said: "Can you raise the limit if I cover it behind the line?"

The man glanced at a tall well-dressed youth behind him for confirmation, nodded.

Kells took a wad of bills out of his trouser pocket and put two hundred-dollar bills down behind the line. Dickinson looked up and his bleary, heavy-lidded eyes came gradually to focus on Kells.

He said, "Hello there," very heartily. Then he looked as if he were trying hard to remember, said: "Kells! How are ya, boy?"

At mention of Kells' name it became very quiet for a moment.

Kells said: "I'm fine."

The little pimpled man rolled.

The dice man said: "Six—an easy one. . . . He will or he won't. . . . Nine pays the field. . . . Six—right. . . ."

The change man picked up Kells' two hundred-dollar bills, tossed them down beside Dickinson's bet.

Dickinson grinned. He said: "Bet it."

Kells took a thousand-dollar note from his breast pocket, put it down behind the line.

Dickinson said: "Better lay off—I'm right. . . ."

"Get down on the bill." Kells smiled faintly, narrowly.

"Damned if I won't." Dickinson counted his money on the table and the money in his hand: "Four hundred, six, eight, nine, a thousand, thousand one hundred an' thirty. Tap me."

The tall young man said: "Hurry up, gentlemen—you're holding up the game."

Several men wandered over from the other table. The little man holding the dice box said:

"Jesus! I don't want . . ."

Kells was counting out the additional hundred and thirty dollars.

Dickinson said: "Roll."

"Eleven—the winner."

The change man picked up Kells' money, cut off a twenty

64

for the house, threw the rest down in front of Dickinson.

The little man raked in the few dollars he had won for himself, walked away.

The dice man picked up the box.

Kells said: "Got enough?"

"Hell, no! I'll bet it all on my own roll." Dickinson held out his hand for the box.

"Make it snappy, boys." The tall young man frowned, nodded briefly at Kells.

Dickinson was checking up on the amount. He said: "Two thousand, two hundred and forty . . ."

Kells put three thousand-dollar notes behind the line. The dice man threw a dozen or more glittering red dice on the table; Dickinson carefully picked out two.

"Get down your bets, men. . . . A new shooter. . . . We take big ones and little ones. . . . Come, don't come, hard way, and in the field. . . . Bet 'em either way. . . ."

Dickinson was shaking the box gently, tenderly, near his ear. He rolled.

"Three—that's a bad one. . . ."

Kells picked up his three notes; the change man raked up the bills in front of Dickinson, counted them into a stack, cut off one and handed the rest to Kells.

"Next man. . . . Get down on the next lucky shooter, boys. . . ."

Kells folded the bills and stuck them into his pocket.

Dickinson looked at the tall young man, said: "Let me take five hundred, Les."

The young man looked at him with soft unseeing eyes, turned and walked away. Kells gestured with his head and went over to a round green-covered table out of the circle of light. Dickinson followed him, they sat down.

Kells said: "Can you get the paper out by tomorrow morning?"

Dickinson was fumbling through his pockets, brought out a dark brown pint bottle. He took out the cork, held the bottle toward Kells. "Wha' for?"

Kells shook his head but Dickinson shoved the bottle into his hands. Kells took a drink, handed it back.

"Bellmann was fogged tonight and I want to give it a big spread."

"The hell you say!" Dickinson stared blankly at Kells. "Well, wha'dy' know about that!" Then he seemed to remember Kells' question. "Sure."

Kells said: "Let's go."

"Wait a minute. Let's have another drink."

They drank.

Dickinson said: "Listen. Wha'dy' think happened to-night? Somebody called me up an' offered me ten grand, cold turkey, to ditch Lee."

"Ditch him, how?"

"I don't know. They said all I had to do was gum up the works some way so that the paper wouldn't come out. They said I'd get five in cash in the mail tomorrow, an' the rest after the primaries."

"What did you say?"

"I said, 'Listen, sister, Lee Fenner's been a damned good friend to me.' I said—"

Kells said: "Sister?"

"Yeah. It was a broad."

They got up and went through the semidarkness to the little room, out and downstairs to the street. It was raining very hard. Dickinson said he had a car; Kells paid off the cab and they went into the vacant lot alongside the building.

Dickinson's car was a Ford coupé; he finally found his keys and opened the door. Then a bright spotlight was switched on in a car at the curb. There was a sharp choked roar and something bit into Kells' leg, into his side. Dickinson stumbled, fell down on his knees on the running board; his face and the upper part of his body sagged forward to the floor of the car. He lay still.

*   *   *   *   *

Kells lay down in the mud beside the car and drew up his knees and he could taste blood in his mouth. His teeth were sunk savagely, deeply into his lower lip, and there were jagged wires of pain in his brain, jagged wires in his side.

He knew that it had been a shotgun, and he lay in the mud with rain whipping his face, wondered if Dickinson was dead, waited for the gun to cough again.

Then the spotlight went out and Kells could hear the car being shifted into gear; he twisted his head a little and saw it pass through the light near the corner—a Cadillac.

He crawled up onto the running board of the Ford and shook Dickinson a little, and then he slowly, painfully, pushed Dickinson up into the car—slowly.

He pressed the knob that unlocked the opposite door and limped around the car and crawled into the driver's seat. He could feel blood on his side; blood pounded through his head, his eyes. He pried the keys out of Dickinson's hand and started the motor. Dickinson was an inert heap beside him. He groaned, coughed in a curious dry way.

Kells said: "All right, boy. We'll fix it up in a minute."

Dickinson coughed again in the curious way that was like a laugh. He tried to sit up, fell forward and his head banged against the windshield. Kells pulled him back into the seat and drove out of the lot, turned east on Santa Monica.

Dickinson tried to say something, groped with one hand in the side pocket. He finally gave it up, managed to gasp: "Gun—here."

Kells said: "Sit still."

They went down Santa Monica Boulevard very fast, turned north on La Brea. Kells stopped halfway up the block and felt in Dickinson's pocket for the bottle, but it had been broken, the pocket was full of wet glass.

They went up La Brea to Franklin, over Franklin to Cahuenga, up Cahuenga and Irish to Cullen's house.

Kells' side and leg had become numb. He got out of the car as quickly as be could, limped up the steps. Cullen answered the first ring, stood in the doorway looking elaborately disgusted, said: "Again?"

Kells said: "Give me a hand, Willie. Hurry up." He started back down the steps.

"No! God damn you and your jams!"

Kells turned and stared at Cullen expressionlessly, and then he went on down the steps. Cullen followed him, muttering; they got Dickinson out of the car, carried him up into the house.

Cullen was breathing heavily. He asked: "Why the hell don't you take him to the Receiving Hospital?"

"I've been mixed up in five shootings in the last thirty-two hours." Kells went to the telephone, grinned over his shoulder at Cullen. "It's like old times—one more and they'll hang me on principle."

"Haven't you got any other friends? This place was lousy with coppers *yesterday.*"

"Wha's the matter, darling?"

Kells and Cullen turned, looked at the stairway. Eileen, Cullen's girl, was standing halfway down. She swayed back and forth, put her hand unsteadily on the banister. She was very drunk. She was naked.

She drawled: "Hello, Gerry."

Cullen said: "Go back upstairs and put on your clothes, slut!" He said it very loudly.

Kells laughed, said: "Call Doc Janis—will you, Willie?" He limped to the door, looked down at his torn, muddy, bloodstained clothes. "And loan me a coat, Willie—or I'll get wet."

* * * * *

A black touring car with the side curtains drawn was parked in the reserved space in front of the Knickerbocker. Kells had been about to park across the street; he slowed down, blinked at it. The engine was running and there was a man at the wheel. It was a Cadillac.

He stepped on the throttle, careened around the corner, parked in front of the library. He jumped out and took the revolver out of the side pocket, slipped it into the pocket of Cullen's big coat; he turned up the deep collar and hurried painfully back across the street, down an alley to a service entrance of the hotel.

The boy in the elevator said: "Well, I guess I was right—I guess it's going to rain all night."

Kells said: "Uh huh."

"Tch tch tch." The boy shook his head sadly.

"Has Mister Fenner had any visitors since I left?"

"No, sir—I don't think so. Not many people in and out tonight. There was three gentlemen went up to nine little while ago. They was drunk, I guess." He slid the door open. "Ten, sir."

Kells said: "Thank you."

He listened at the door of ten-sixteen, heard no sound, rang the bell and stood close to the wall with the revolver in his hand. The inner hallway was narrow—the door would have to be opened at least halfway before he could be seen.

It opened almost at once, slowly. A yellow-white face

took form in the darkness, and Kells stepped in to the doorway. He held the revolver belly-high in front of him. The yellow-white face faded backwards as Kells went in until it was the black outline of a man's head against orange light of the living room, until it was the figure of a short Latin standing with his back against the wall at one side of the door, his arms stretched out.

Beyond him, Fenner and Beery kneeled on the floor, their faces to the wall. On the other side of the room O'Donnell stood with a great blue automatic leveled at Kells' chest. O'Donnell was bareheaded and a white bulge of gauze and cotton plastered across his scalp. His mouth was open and he breathed through it slowly, audibly. Except for the sharp sound of his breathing, it was entirely still.

Kells said: "I'll bet I can shoot faster than you, Adenoids."

O'Donnell didn't say anything. His pale eyes glittered in a sick face and the big automatic was glistening and steady in his fat pink hand.

Fenner leaned forward, put his head against the wall. Beery turned slowly and looked at Kells. The Mexican was motionless, bright-eyed.

Then Beery said, "Look out!" and something dull and terrible crashed against the back of Kells' head, there was dull and terrible blackness. It was filled with thunder and smothering blue, something hot and alive pulsed in Kells' hand. He fell.

* * * * *

There was light that hurt his eyes very much, even when they were closed. Someone was throwing water in his face. He said: "Stop that, damn it—you're getting me wet!"

Beery said: "Sh—easy."

Kells opened his eyes a little. "The place is backwards."

"This is the one next door, one across the airshaft where Fenner's stick-up men were stashed. Fenner had the key." Beery spoke very quietly.

"God! My head. How did I get in here?"

Beery said: "Papa carried you." He stood up and went to the door for a minute, came back and sat down. "And what a piece of business! You were out on your feet—absolutely cold—squeezed that iron, one, two, three, four, five, six—like that. One in the wall about six inches above my head, five in baby-face."

"That was O'Donnell." Kells closed his eyes and moved his head a little. Beery nodded.

"Who hit me?"

"Rose."

Kells looked interested. "What with—a piano?"

"A vase. . . ."

"Vahze."

Beery said: "A vase—a big one out of the bedroom. I don't think he had a gun."

"Would you mind beginning at the beginning?" Kells closed his eyes again.

"After you left, Fenner and Gowdy sat there like a couple bumps on a log, afraid to crack in front of me."

Kells nodded carefully, held his head in his hands.

"After a while, Gowdy got bored and went home—he lives around the corner. I was sucking up a lot of red-eye, having a swell time. Then about five minutes before you got here the bell rang and Fenner went to the door, backed in with Rose and O'Donnell and the spiggoty. O'Donnell and the spick was snowed to the eyes. Rose said, 'What did Kells get from that gal that bumped Bellmann, and where is it?' Fenner went into a nose dive—he was scared wet, anyway. They made us get down on the floor—"

Kells laughed, said: "You looked like a couple communicants."

"—and Rose frisked both of us and started tearing up the furniture. Some way or other I got the idea that whether he found what he was looking for or not, we weren't going to tell about it afterwards."

Beery paused, lighted a cigaret, went on quietly: "Rose was sore as hell, and O'Donnell and the greaser were leaking C out of their ears. The greaser kept fingering a chiv in his belt—you know: the old noiseless ear-to-ear trick."

Kells said: "Maybe. They popped Dickinson and me outside Ansel's. If they're that far in the open maybe they'd want to get Fenner too."

"And Beery—the innocent bystander. . . ."

"I doubt it, Shep. I don't think Rose would have come along if it was a kill."

"Well, anyway—he'd got around to the bedroom when you rang. He switched out the light and waited in there in the dark. You came in and went into your Wild West act with baby-face, and Rose came behind you and took a bead on your skull with the vase—vahze. Then he and the greaser scrammed—quick."

Kells reached suddenly into his inside pocket, then took his hand out, sighed. "Didn't he fan me?"

"No. I grabbed O'Donnell's gun when he fell—anyway, I think Rose was too scared to think about that."

Kells said: "Go on."

Beery looked immensely superior. "Well, the old rapid-fire Beery brain got to work. I figured that you had to be out of there quick and I remembered what you'd said about this place next door. Fenner was about to go into his fit—I got the key from him and talked about thirty seconds' worth of sense, and carried you in here—and the gun." He nodded at the revolver on the couch beside Kells. "Where's Fenner now?"

"Over at the Station filing murder charges against Rose and the greaser."

Kells said: "That's swell."

"The housedick and a bunch of coppers and a lot of neighbors who had heard the barrage got here at about the same time. It was the fastest police action I've ever seen; must have been one of the radio cars. I listened through the airshaft. Fenner had pulled himself together, told a beautiful story about Rose and O'Donnell and the Mex crashing in, O'Donnell getting it in an argument with Rose."

Beery mashed out his cigaret. "He's telling it over at headquarters now—or maybe he's on his way back. You've been out about a half-hour."

Kells sat up unsteadily, said: "Give me a drink of water." He bent over and very carefully rolled up his trouser leg, examined his injured leg.

A little later there was a tap at the door and Beery opened it, let Fenner in.

Fenner looked very tired. He said: "How are you, Gerry?"

"I'm fine, Lee—how are you?" Kells grinned.

71

"Terrible—terrible! I can't stand this kind of thing." Fenner sat down.

"Maybe you'd better take a trip, after all." Kells smiled faintly, picked up the revolver. "Things are going to be more in the open from now on, I guess—I'll have to carry a gun." He looked down at the revolver.

"By God, I'll get a permit for a change," he said: "Can you fix that up?"

Fenner nodded wearily. "I guess so."

"And Lee, we made a deal tonight—I mean early—the twenty-five grand, you know. I'm going to handle the stuff, of course; but in the interests of my client, Miss Granquist, I'll have to consummate the sale."

Fenner looked at the floor.

"A check'll be all right."

Fenner nodded. "I'll go in and make it out," he said. "Then I'll have to say goodnight—I'm all in."

"That'll be all right."

Fenner went out and closed the door.

Kells sat looking at the door for a moment and then he said: "Shep—you're the new editor of the *Coast Guardian*. How do you like that?"

"Lousy. I don't carry enough insurance."

"You'll be all right. A hundred a week and all the advertising you can sell on the side."

"When do I start?"

"Right now. I parked Dickinson up at Bill Cullen's. I'll drop you there and you can get the details from him—if he's conscious. I'll turn the, uh—data over to you. . . ."

Beery rubbed his eyes, yawned. He smiled a little and said: "Oh well, what the hell. I guess I'm beginning to like it."

Kells looked at his wrist. "The bastards smashed my watch—what time is it?"

"Twelve-two."

Kells picked up the telephone and called a Hempstead number. He said: "Hello, baby . . . Sure . . . Have you got any ham and eggs? . . . Have you got some absorbent cotton and bandages and iodine? . . . That's fine, I'll be up in about ten minutes . . . I've been on a party."

Doctor Janis looked wiser than any one man could possibly be. His head was as round and white and bare as a cue ball; his nose was a long bony hook and his eyes were pale, immensely shrewd.

He jabbed forceps gently into Kells' leg, said: "Hurt?"

Kells stuck out his lips, shook his head slightly. "No. Not very much."

"You're a damned liar!" Janis straightened, glared.

Bright sun beat through the wide east windows; the big instrument case against one white wall glistened. Kells was half lying on a small operating table. He stared at the bright point of sunlight on the wall, tried not to think about the leg.

"God deliver me from a sadistic doctor," he said.

Janis grinned, bent again over the leg, probed deeper. "That was a dandy." He held a tiny twisted chunk of lead up in the forceps' point, exhibited it proudly. "Now you know how a rabbit feels."

"Now I know how it feels to be a mother. You're as proud of a few shot as a *good* doctor would be of triplets."

Janis chuckled, jabbed again with the forceps.

At a little after eight-thirty, Kells left Janis's office in the Harding Building. It had rained all night; the air was sharp, clear. He limped across Hollywood Boulevard to a small jewelry store, left his watch to be repaired and asked that they send it to him at the hotel as soon as possible. He went out and bought a paper and got a cab, said, "Ambassador," leaned back and spread the paper. Then he sat up very straight.

A headline read: WOMAN IN BELLMANN KILLING ESCAPES.

He glanced out the window at a tangle of traffic as the cab curved into Vine Street; then leaned back again slowly, read the story:

Early this morning, Miss S. Granquist, alleged by police to be the self-confessed slayer of John R. Bellmann, prominent philanthropist and reformer, was "kidnaped" from Detectives Breen and Rail after the car in which they were taking her from the Hollywood Police Station to the County Jail

had been forced to the curb near Temple Street and Cor-
onado, crashed into a fire plug. Officer Breen was slightly
injured, removed to the Receiving Hospital. Rail described
the "abductors" as, "eight or nine heavily armed and des-
perate men in a cream-colored coupé." He neglected to
explain how "eight or nine" men and a woman got away in
a coupé. Our motor-car manufacturers would be interested
in how that was done. It is opportune that another example
of the inefficiency of our police department occurs almost on
the eve of the municipal primaries. The voters . . .

Kells folded the paper, knocked on the glass and told
the driver to make it fast. They cut over Melrose to Normandie, out of the heavy traffic, over Normandie to Wil-
shire Boulevard and into the big parking circle of the
Ambassador.

Kells told the driver to wait, hurried up to his room and
changed clothes. He called the desk, was told that Mister
Beery had called twice, called Beery back at the Hayward
Hotel downtown. The room line was busy. He took a long
drink and went back down and got into the cab. It took
twenty-five minutes to get through the traffic on lower Seventh Street to the Hayward.

Fenner opened the door of the small outer room on the
fourth floor; they went through to the larger bedroom.

Kells said: "You're down early, Lee."

Fenner glanced at the rolled newspaper in Kells' hand,
nodded, smiled wanly.

"Where's Beery?" Kells took off his hat and coat.

Fenner sat down on the bed. "He went over to the print
shop about an hour ago. He ought to be back pretty soon."

Kells sat down carefully.

Fenner asked: "How's the leg?"

"Doc Janis picked eleven shot out of it like plucking
petals off a daisy. It came out odd—he loves me." Kells
unrolled, unfolded the paper, looked over it at Fenner. "Do
you know anything about this?"

"I do not." Fenner said it very quietly, very emphatically.

"What do you think?"

"Rose."

Kells stared at Fenner steadily. He moved his fingers on

74

the arm of the chair as though running scales. He said: "What for?"

"She's crossed him up all the way—he's the kind of a crazy guy that would take a long chance to get even."

Kells sat staring blankly at Fenner for perhaps a minute. Then he said slowly: "I want you to call Gowdy—everybody you can reach who might have a line on it. . . ."

Fenner got up and went to the phone. He called several numbers, spoke softly, quietly.

After a little while the other door opened and someone came through the outer room. It was Beery. He said: "We can't get it on the newsstands before noon."

"That'll be all right."

Kells was still sitting deep in the big chair. Fenner was at the telephone. Beery took off his coat and hat, flopped down on the bed.

"Maybe I can get a couple hours' snooze," he said.

Fenner hung up the receiver and looked at Kells. "You might pick up something at the Bronx, out on Central Avenue. It's a nigger cabaret run by a man named Sheedy. Rose is supposed to be a partner—he was seen there last night."

"Who's Sheedy?"

Beery said: "A big dinge—used to be in pictures. . . ."

"You know him?"

"A little."

"Get on the phone and see if you can locate him. He wouldn't be at his joint this time of day."

Beery sighed, sat up. "The law's looking for Rose too, Gerry," he said. "You're not going to get anything out of any of these boys."

Kells half smiled, inclined his head toward the phone. Then he stood up.

"If that son of a bitch got her—which is a long shot"—he looked sideways at Fenner—"he'll give her everything in the book. I got her into it—and by God! I'll get her out if I have to turn the rap back on Lee and let the whole play slide." He turned, went to one of the windows. "And if Rose *did* get her and lets her have it I'll spread his guts from here to Caliente."

Beery got up and went to the phone. "You're getting plenty dramatic about a gal you turned up yourself," he said.

Kells turned from the window and looked at Beery, and his eyes were cold, his mouth was partly open, faintly smiling.

He said: "Right."

*   *   *   *   *

Sheedy couldn't be located.

Fenner got Officer Rail on the phone and Kells talked to him. Rail said he couldn't identify any of the men who had taken Granquist; he thought one of them was crippled, wore a steel brace on his leg. He wasn't sure.

Kells called Rose's place on Fifth Street; there was no answer. He called the Biltmore, was told that Rose hadn't been in for two days; Mrs. Rose was out of town.

Beery napped for an hour. Kells and Fenner sat in the outer room; Fenner read a detective-story magazine and Kells sat deep in a big chair, stared out the window. Hanline stopped in for a minute. He said he'd speak to one of the bellboys downstairs, send up a bottle.

At a little after ten-thirty the phone rang. Fenner answered it, called Kells.

A man's high-pitched voice said: "I have been authorized to offer you fifteen thousand dollars for the whole issue of the *Guardian*, together with the plates and all data used in its make-up."

Kells said, "I don't know what you're talking about," hung up. He told Fenner to hurry down to the switchboard, try to trace the call; waited for the phone to ring again. It did almost immediately. The man's voice said: "It will be very much to your advantage to talk business, Mister Kells."

"Who's your authority?"

"The Bellmann estate."

Kells said: "If you know where Miss Granquist is and can produce her within the next half-hour, I'll talk to you."

There was a long silence at the other end of the line. Then the man said: "Wait a minute." After a little while a woman's voice said: "Gerry! For God's sake get me out of this! . . ." The voice trailed off as if she had been dragged away from the phone. The man's voice said: "Well?"

Fenner came in, nodded to Kells.

Kells said: "Okay. Bring her here." He hung up.

The phone rang again but he didn't answer. He sat grinning at Fenner.

Fenner said excitedly: "West Adams—about a block west of Figueroa."

"That wasn't even a good imitation of the baby." Kells stood up. "But maybe they'll come here and try to do business on that angle. That'll be swell."

"But we'd better get out there, hadn't we?"

Kells said: "What for? They haven't got her or they wouldn't take a chance faking her voice. They'll be here—and I'll lay ten to one they don't know any more about where Rose and the kid are than we do."

Kells went back to his chair by the window. "I told Shep to plant some men at the print shop in case there's trouble there. Did he?" Fenner nodded.

There was a knock at the door; Fenner said, "Come in," and a boy came in with a bottle of whiskey and three tall glasses of ice on a tray. He put the tray on a table; Fenner gave him some change and he went out and closed the door.

At twenty minutes after eleven a Mister Woodward was announced. Fenner went into the bedroom, closed the door.

Woodward turned out to be a small yellow-haired man, wearing tortoise-shell glasses; about thirty-five. He sat down at Kells' invitation, declined a drink.

He said: "Of course we couldn't bring Miss Granquist here. She's being sought by the police and that would be too dangerous. She'll be turned over to you, together with a certified check for fifteen thousand dollars, as soon as the issue of the *Guardian*, the plates and the copy are turned over to us."

Kells said: "What the hell kind of a cheap outfit are you? The stuff's worth that much simply as state's evidence—let alone its political value to your people."

"I know—I know." Woodward bobbed his head up and down. "The fact of the matter is, Mister Kells—my people are up against it for cash. They'll know how to show their appreciation in other ways, however."

"What other ways?"

"Certain political concessions after election—uh—you

know." Woodward glanced nervously at his watch. "And it is imperative that you make a decision quickly."

Kells said: "I'm not in politics. I want the dough. Lay fifty thousand on the line and show me Miss Granquist"—he looked at his watch, smiled—"and it is imperative that *you* make a decision quickly."

Woodward stood up. "Very well, Mister Kells," he said. His voice had risen in pitch to the near-falsetto of the telephone conversation. "What you ask is impossible. I'll say good-day."

He started toward the door and Kells said: "Hold on a minute." The big automatic that had been O'Donnell's glittered dully in his hand. "Sit down."

Woodward's blue eyes were wide behind his glasses. He went back toward the chair.

Kells said: "No. Over by the phone."

Woodward smiled weakly, sat down at the telephone stand.

"Now you'd better call up your parties and tell them everything's all right—that we made a deal."

Woodward was looking at the rug. He pursed his lips, shook his head slowly.

"There's a direct line in the other room," Kells went on, "if you'd rather not make it through the switchboard."

Woodward didn't move except to shake his head slowly; he stared at the floor, smiled a little.

"Hurry up." Kells stood up.

Then the phone in the bedroom rang; Kells could faintly hear Beery say "Hello." It was quiet for a moment and then the bedroom door opened and Fenner stood in the doorway looking back at Beery.

Beery said: "You sure? . . . Just the press and the forms. . . . All out? . . . All right, I'll be right over." The receiver clicked and Beery came into the doorway. He glanced at Woodward, grinned crookedly at Kells.

"They blew up the joint," he said. "But nearly all the stuff was out. A hand press and a couple of linotypes were cracked up and one guy's got a piece of iron in his shoulder, but they discovered it in time and got everybody else and the sheets out. The originals are in the safe."

He struck an attitude, declaimed: "The first issue of *The Coast Guardian; A Political Weekly for Thinking People,* is on the stands."

Kells turned slowly, sat down. He looked steadily at Woodward for a while and then he said: "As representative of the Bellmann estate"—he paused, coughed gently—"do you think you're strong enough to beat charges of coercion, conspiracy to defeat justice, dynamiting, abduction—a few more that any half-smart attorney can figure out?".

Woodward kept his eyes down. "That was a stall about the girl. We haven't got her, and we don't know where Rose is. . . ."

"So Rose *has* got her?"

Woodward looked up, spoke hesitantly: "I don't know."

"If you've got any ideas, now's a swell time to spill them."

Woodward glanced at Beery, Fenner, back to Kells. "My people don't want to have anything to do with Rose," he said. "He's wanted for murder and if he's caught he'll get the works." He smiled again, went on slowly: "He called up this morning and said *you* shot O'Donnell—said he could prove it. . . ."

Fenner laughed quietly.

Kells said: "Where did he call from?"

Woodward shook his head. "Don't know."

Beery had gone back into the bedroom. He came into the doorway again, pulling on his coat. "I'll be back in about an hour, Gerry," he said. He poured himself a short drink, swallowed it and went out making faces.

Kells asked Woodward: "Where can I find you?"

Woodward hesitated a moment. "I've got an office in the Dell Building—the number's in the book."

"You can go."

Woodward got up and said: "Good-day, sir." He nodded at Fenner, went out.

Kells took Fenner's twenty-five-thousand-dollar check out of his inside coat pocket. He unfolded it and looked at it for a minute and then he said: "Let's go over to the bank and have this certified."

They went out together.

Kells slept most of the afternoon. Doctor Janis stopped by at seven. The leg was pretty stiff.

Janis said. "You ought to stay in a couple days, anyway. You're damned lucky it was the edge of the fan got you— Dickinson got the middle. . . ."

Kells asked: "How is he?"

"He'll be all right. He's too tough."

Janis put on his coat and hat and went to the door. "You had a break," he said—"don't press it." He went out.

Kells telephoned Fenner. There had been several steers on Rose—all of them bad. Sheedy hadn't been located. The Mexican who had been with Rose was probably Abalos, from Frisco. He lived at a small hotel on Main street which was being watched. Reilly was being tailed.

Beery came up about eight. "Everything's lovely," he said. "All the evening papers carried the *Guardian* stuff— I'm the fair-haired boy at the *Chronicle*." He put down his glass. "You want me to keep the *Chronicle* job too, don't you?"

Kells said: "Sure."

Beery stooped over the low table and mixed himself a drink. "I'm going to the fights. Swell card."

"So am I."

Beery squinted over his shoulder. "You'd better stay in the hay," he said.

Kells swung up, sat on the edge of the bed. "Got your ducats?'

"Yeah. I was going to take the wife."

"Sure—we'll take her. Call up and see if you can get three together, close." Kells limped into the bathroom, turned on the shower.

Beery sat tinkling ice against the sides of his glass. When Kells turned off the shower Beery yelled: "The old lady don't want to go anyway."

Kells stood in the bathroom door, grinning.

Beery looked up at him and then down at his glass. "I guess she don't like you very well." He picked up the phone and asked for a Hollywood number.

Kells disappeared into the bathroom again, and when he came out Beery smiled happily, said: "Okay. She'd rather go to a picture show."

* * * * *

The seats were fifth row, ringside—two seats off the aisle. The second preliminary was in its last round when Kells and Beery squeezed past a very fat man in the aisle seat, sat down.

The preliminary ended in a draw and the lights flared on. Kells nodded to several acquaintances, and Beery leaned forward, talked to a friend of his in the row ahead. He introduced the man to Kells: Brand, feature sports writer for an Eastern syndicate.

Kells had been looking at his program, asked: "What's the price on Gilroy?"

"The boys were offering three to two before dinner—very little business. I'll lay two to one on Shane."

Gilroy was a New York Negro, a heavyweight who had been at the top of his class for a while. Too much living, and racial discrimination—too few fights—had softened him. The dopesters said he'd lost everything he ever had, was on the skids. Shane was a tough kid from Texas. He was reputed to have a right-hand punch that more than made up for his lack of experience.

Kells remembered Gilroy—from Harlem—had known him well, liked him. He said: "I'll take five hundred of that."

Brand looked at him very seriously, nodded.

Beery looked disgusted. He leaned toward Kells, muttered: "For God's sake, Gerry, they're grooming Shane for a title shot. Do you think they're going to let an unpopular boogie like Gilroy get anywhere?"

Kells said: "He used to be very good—he can't have gone as bad as they say in a year. I've only seen Shane once and I thought he was lousy. . . ."

"He won, didn't he?"

"Uh huh."

Beery was looking at Kells sideways with wide hard eyes.

The man sitting with Brand turned around and drawled: "You don't happen to have any more Gilroy money, do you?"

"Sure."

The man said: "I'll give you eighteen hundred for a grand."

Kells nodded.

Beery looked like he was going to fall off his chair. He muttered expletives under his breath.

A man crawled into the ring, followed by two Filipinos with their seconds. The house lights dimmed.

"Ladies and gentlemen . . . Six rounds . . . In this corner—Johnny Sanga . . . a hundred an' thirty-four . . ."

Kells said: "I'll be back in a minute." He got up and squeezed out past the fat man.

At the head of the corridor that led to the dressing rooms a uniformed policeman said: "You can't go any farther, buddy."

Kells looked at him coldly. "I'm Mister Olympic—I own this place." He twisted a bill around his finger, stepped close and shoved it into the copper's hand, went on.

Gilroy was sitting on the edge of a rubbing table while a squat heavily sweatered youth taped his hands. A florid bejeweled Greek sat in a chair tilted back against the wall, smoking a short green cigar. He stood up when Kells opened the door, said: "You can't come in here, mister."

Gilroy looked up and his face split in a huge grin. "Well Ah'll be switch'—Mistah Kells!" He got up and came towards Kells, held out his half-taped hand.

Kells smiled, shook hands. "H'are ya, Lonny?"

Gilroy's grin was enormous. He said: "Sit down—sit down."

Kells shook his head, leaned against the table. He glanced at the Greek and at the boy who had resumed taping the big Negro's hand. He looked at Gilroy, said: "You win?"

"Shuah—shuah." Gilroy's grin was a shade less easy. "Shuah, Ah win."

Kells kept looking at him. Gilroy looked at the Greek, then back at Kells. He shook his head slightly. "How long you been out hyah, Mistah Kells?"

Kells didn't answer. He stared at Gilroy vacantly. The

Greek looked at Gilroy and then glanced icily at Kells, went out of the room. The squat youth kept on taping Gilroy's hand mechanically.

Gilroy said: "No. Ah don't win." He said it very softly.

"How much are you getting?"

Gilroy's face had become very serious. "Nothin'," he said. "Not a nickel."

Kells rubbed the back of one hand with the palm of the other.

Gilroy went on: "Not a nickel—but Ah get plenty if Ah don't throw it. . . ."

"What are you talking about?"

The boy finished one hand. Gilroy flexed it, looked at the floor.

"They've put the feah o' God in me, Mistah Kells. If Ah win, Ah don't go home tonight—maybe."

Kells turned to face him squarely, said: "You mean you're going to take a dive for nothing."

"If that's the way you want to put it—yes, sah."

The boy started on the other hand. Gilroy went on: "Ah been gettin' letters an' phone calls an' warnin's for a week. . . ."

"Who from?"

"Don't know." Gilroy shook his head slowly.

Kells glanced at his watch. He said: "Do you figure you owe me anything, Lonny?"

Gilroy looked at him, and his eyes were big, liquid. "Shuah," he said—"shuah—Ah remembah."

"This is *my* town, now. I want you to go in and win, if you can. I'll have a load of protection here by the time you get in the ring—you can stick with me afterwards." Kells looked at him very intently. "This is important."

Gilroy was entirely still for a moment. He stared at his hands. Then he nodded slowly without looking up.

Kells said: "I'll be back here afterwards."

He went out of the room, closed the door. He found a telephone, called Fenner. Fenner wasn't in, he had the call switched to Hanline's room; when Hanline answered, Kells told him to send the two best muscle men he could locate to the entrance of Section R, Olympic Arena, quickly. Hanline said: "Sure—what's it all about?" Kells said: "Nothing.

What's the use of having an organization if I don't use it?"

On the way back to his seat Kells saw Fay. They walked together to an archway through which they could see the ring. The Filipinos were locked in a slow and measured dance; the electric indicator above the ring read: Round FIVE.

Kells asked: "Who's interested in Shane?"

Fay shrugged. "His mother, I suppose . . ."

"Is this so-called syndicate building him up?"

"Sure."

Kells pointed a finger, jabbed it at Fay's chest "And who the hell is the syndicate?"

Fay said: "Rose—and whoever his backers are."

Kells looked at the ring. "Your guess is as good as mine. Get down on Gilroy." He walked away with an extravagantly mysterious and meaningful look over his shoulder.

Back in his seat Kells tapped Brand's shoulder. "If you gentlemen would like to get out from under," he said, "you can copper those bets now."

Brand turned to Kells' wide smile. His drawling friend was engrossed in the last waltz of the Filipinos.

"I have *information* . . ." Kells widened his smile.

Brand shook his head, matched his smile, said: "No—Shane's good enough for me."

"That's what I thought. That's the reason I made the offer."

Beery was yelling at one of the Filipinos. He glanced at Kells without expression, shouted at the ring: "Ask him what he's doing after the show."

The last preliminary was declared a draw. The semi-wind-up came up: six rounds—a couple of dark smart flyweights, one on his way to a championship. It was a pretty good fight but it was the favorite's all the way.

The main event followed almost immediately. The announcer climbed into the ring—the referee, Shane, Gilroy, a knot of seconds. Shane got a big hand. Gilroy got a pretty good reception too—the black belt was well represented and Gilroy was well liked. The disk was tossed for corners, taping was examined and the referee's instructions passed.

"Ladies and gentlemen . . . Ten rounds . . . In this corner—Arthur Shane—the Texas Cyclone . . . Two hundred an' eight pounds . . . In this corner—Lon Gilroy . . . A hundred ninety-six. . . ."

The announcer and seconds scrambled out of the ring. Gilroy and Shane touched gloves, turned toward their corners. At the gong Shane whirled, almost ran across the ring. Gilroy looked faintly surprised, waited, calmly ducked Shane's wild right hook. They exchanged short jabs to the body and Shane straightened a long one to Gilroy's jaw.

Shane's hair was so blond it was almost white. It stuck straight up in a high pompadour above his round pink face, flopped back and forth as he moved his head. He was thick, looked more than his two hundred and eight pounds. Gilroy had put on fat in the year since Kells had seen him in action, but it looked hard. His rich chocolate-brown body still sloped to a narrow waist, straight well-muscled legs. He looked pretty good.

Shane came in fast again; Gilroy backed against the ropes, came out and under Shane's right—they clinched. The referee stepped between them, and Gilroy clipped Shane's chin as he sidled away. They exchanged short jabs to the head and body, fell into another clinch. Gilroy brought both hands up hard to Shane's body. Shane danced away, came in fast again and snapped Gilroy's head back with a long right. They were stalling, waiting for the other to lead at the bell. The round was even.

The second and third rounds were slow—the second Shane's by a shade, the third even.

Shane came out fast in the fourth, grazed Gilroy's jaw with the long right, drove his left hard into Gilroy's stomach. Gilroy straightened up and his mouth was open; Shane stepped a little to one side, took Gilroy's weak counter on his shoulder and hooked his right to Gilroy's unprotected jaw. There was a snap and Gilroy sank down on his knees. The crowd roared. Several people stood up.

Gilroy took a count of eight, got up grinning broadly. He ducked Shane's wild uppercut, stepped inside and pounded Shane's body, but his punches lacked steam. The muscles of his face were taut, his eyes big—he had been hurt. They clinched. The round was Shane's.

Gilroy held on during the first part of the fifth, but snapped out of it in time to smack Shane around considerably before the bell. Shane was tiring a little. It should have been Gilroy's round but was declared even.

The sixth and seventh were Gilroy's by a small margin. He seemed to have recovered all his speed; Shane brought the fight to him, made a good show of rushing but it didn't mean much. Gilroy took everything Shane had to give—fought deliberately, hard, well.

The rounds stood two apiece, three even. Kells watched Shane between the seventh and eighth, decided that whatever the fix had been, he wasn't in on it. He looked worried, but it didn't look like the kind of worry one would feel at being double-crossed. His backers had evidently let him believe that he would win or lose fairly. As a matter of fact it hadn't been bribery or a frameup, strictly speaking—they'd simply scared Gilroy and it had almost worked.

Brand turned around, smiled uncomfortably.

Kells whispered to Beery: "The eighth does it." He looked at Gilroy. Gilroy was lying back, breathing deeply. He raised his head and stared intently at the faces around the ring. Kells tried to catch his eye but the seconds were crawling out of the ring, the gong sounded.

Shane rushed again and Gilroy stood very still, blocked Shane's haymaker and swung his left in a long loop to Shane's head. Shane fell as if he had been hit with an axe. Gilroy looked down at him wonderingly for a second, shuffled to a neutral corner. Everyone stood up. The referee was counting but he couldn't be heard above the roar; his arm moved up and down and his lips moved.

Shane sat up, got unsteadily to his feet. Gilroy came in and put out his two hands and pushed him. Gilroy was smiling self-consciously. Shane was all right; he shook his head and went after Gilroy, and Gilroy cuffed him on the side of the head, jabbed straight left to his face. Shane stepped in close and swung his right in a wide up-and-down circle, hit Gilroy a good ten inches below the belt, hard.

Gilroy folded up slowly. He held his hands over the middle of his body and bent his knees slowly. His face was twisted with pain. He stumbled forward and straightened up a little and then fell down on his side and drew his knees up.

Shane was leaning against the ropes and his breathing was sharply audible in the momentary silence.

Then the ring filled with people; Gilroy was carried to his corner. The announcer was shouting vainly for silence. One of Shane's seconds held the ropes apart for him; he stared dazedly at the crowd, ducked through the ropes, into the tunnel that led to the dressing rooms.

"Gilroy—on a foul." The announcer made himself faintly heard.

Brand's friend turned around and grinned wryly at Kells, shook his head sadly. "The son of a bitch," he said—"the dirty son of a bitch."

*　*　*　*　*

At the entrance to Section R, Kells almost ran into the fat man who had stuck him up at Fenner's. His tie was sticking out of his high stiff collar at the same cocky angle, his small head was covered by a big, violently plaid cap.

He stared at Kells' shoes, said: "Hanline sent us." He jerked his head at a fairly tall middle-aged man who looked like a prosperous insurance salesman. "This is Denny Faber."

Kells laughed.

The fat one grinned good-naturedly. "I sure slipped up the other night," he said—"the gal cramped my style." He glanced at Beery, looked back at Kells' shoes, went on: "My name is Borg."

Kells introduced Beery. Then the four of them went through the crowd to the dressing rooms.

There were a dozen or more men—mostly Negroes—in the corridor outside Gilroy's room. Kells shouldered through, opened the door. The florid Greek was standing just inside, smiling happily. He poked a finger at Kells.

"I told you we would win—I told you," he said. He turned, frowned at Beery and Borg—Faber had waited outside.

Kells said: "These gentlemen are friends of mine."

They came in behind him.

Gilroy was lying naked on the rubbing table. His face was

87

covered with little beads of sweat. He turned his head, said: "Hello, Mistah Kells."

Kells went over to him "How do you feel?"

"Ah'm all right. The Doc here says it's jus' a scratch"—he grinned with all his face—"jus' a scratch."

The doctor nodded.

Kells turned to Borg, said: "Get a cab and wait outside the little gate, down at the end. . . ." He gestured with his hand.

"We got a car." Borg started toward the door.

"That's fine—we'll be out in a few minutes."

Gilroy sat up slowly, picked up a towel and wiped his face. He said:

"How about a showah, Doc?"

The doctor said it would be all right. He was putting on his coat. Kells took a roll of bills out of his pocket, slipped one off and gave it to the doctor.

Beery was standing near the door. He jerked his head and Kells went over to him. Beery asked quietly: "Brand gave you a check?"

Kells nodded.

"The other guy paid off in cash?"

"Yes."

"Gimme. You run a chance of getting into plenty of excitement tonight. I'm going home—I'd better take care of the bankroll."

"I've got Fenner's check too and somewhere around ten grand soft." Kells smiled, shook his head. "Every time I sock something in a bank something happens so I can't get to it. Something's liable to happen to you. . . ."

"Or you."

"Uh huh—so I'll keep the geetus." Kells went back and sat down on the table.

The Greek began a long and vivid account of why Gilroy was the "coming champion."

"I tell you, Mister Kells—your name is Kells, ain't it?—Lonny is better than Johnson in his flower—in his *flower*. . . ."

Beery said: "I'll call you in the morning." He and the doctor went out together.

Gilroy came out of the shower, dressed. On the way to

the car, Kells asked: "Do you know Sheedy?"

"Vince Sheedy? Shuah." Gilroy stayed close to Kells, watched the people they passed, carefully. "His place is right aroun' the co'nah from my hotel."

"Let's go there and celebrate. I want to meet him."

Borg and Faber were sitting in a big closed car outside the little gate. Beery was in the tonneau.

Kells said: "I thought you were going home."

"Oh, what the hell—I'd just as well come along and see the fireworks—if any." Beery sighed.

Kells and Gilroy got in beside him. Kells leaned forward, spoke to Borg: "Gilroy, here, has had some scare letters. We're going to take care of him for a few days."

Borg said: "Sure."

Gilroy told them how to get to Sheedy's place. Kells watched through the rear window but couldn't spot anyone following them. Traffic was heavy. They went down Sixteenth to Central Avenue, turned south.

The rear entrance to Sheedy's Bronx Club was tricky. They left the car in a parking station, went down a narrow passageway between two buildings. Gilroy knocked at a door in the side of the passageway; it was opened and they went downstairs, through a large kitchen, into a short hallway.

Gilroy said: "There's a front way in, but this is the best because we want a private room"—he looked at Kells for confirmation—"don't we?"

Kells nodded.

Gilroy tried one of the doors in the hallway. It was locked. He tried another, opened it and switched on the light.

The room was small. There was a round table with a red-and-white tablecloth in the middle of the room and there were six or seven chairs and a couch. Gilroy pressed a button near the door.

Borg and Faber sat down and Kells stretched out on the couch. Beery studied the photographs—mostly clipped from "Art Models" magazines—on the walls.

A waiter came and Gilroy told him to get Sheedy.

Sheedy turned out to be a very tall, very yellow skeleton. Dinner clothes hung from his high, pointed shoulders as though the least wind would whip them out like a flat black sail. He nodded to Beery. He said: "I am very happy to meet you, Mister Kells." His accent was very precise. Kells guessed that if the name meant anything special to him he was a remarkable actor.

Gilroy asked: "Was you at the fight, Vince?"

"Yes . . . I lost." Sheedy smiled easily.

Gilroy giggled. "Hot dawg!! 'At serves you right—nex' time you know bettah."

Sheedy raised his brows, nodded sadly.

"Hash us up a load of champagne—" Gilroy made a large gesture. "An' send some gals back to sing us a song."

Sheedy said: "Right away, Lonny"—bowed himself out. He was back in about a minute, asked Kells to come into the hallway. "Some fellows just came in"—he inclined his head toward the front of the place—"asked if Lonny was here. I said no."

"Who are they?"

"Man named Arnie Taylor—a Negro—and three white boys. I don't know them."

Kells said: "Who's Taylor?"

Sheedy shook his head. "I don't think he's a particular friend of Lonny's."

"Where's Rose?" Kells spoke very softly, quickly.

Sheedy looked surprised. Then he smiled slowly. "I'm afraid you've got some wrong ideas."

Kells waited; Sheedy went on: "I haven't the slightest idea."

Kells looked at him sleepily, silently.

Sheedy said: "He was here last night—I haven't seen him since."

"Thanks." Kells turned to go back into the room.

Sheedy caught his shoulder. "Rose and I do a little business together," he said—"that's all." He was smiling slightly, looking very straight at Kells.

Kells said: "Liquor business?"

Sheedy shook his head.

"White stuff?"

Sheedy didn't say anything.

Kells looked at the door to the cabaret, said: "Tell Taylor Lonny's back here."

Sheedy said: "I'm under one indictment here, Mister Kells. If there's any trouble and it gets loud I'll lose my license."

"It won't get loud."

The door to the cabaret opened and a very light-colored Negro with straight blue-black hair came into the hallway. There was a white man behind him, and the white man took a stubby revolver out of his coat pocket.

The Negro said: "Sorry, Vince."

Sheedy put his hands up.

Kells clicked a button-switch on the wall with his elbow but the lights in the hallway stayed on.

The white man stayed at the end of the hallway about ten feet away from them. He was short, with a broad bland childlike face. He held the revolver close to his stomach, pointed indiscriminately at Kells and Sheedy.

Taylor came up to them, felt Kells for a gun.

Sheedy started to speak, and then the room door opened and Gilroy stood outlined against darkness.

He asked: "Wha's the mattah with the lights?"

Taylor turned his head, jerked an automatic out of his belt, swung it toward Gilroy. Kells slammed his open left hand down hard on Taylor's arm and then he got his other arm around Taylor's neck and hugged him back close to the walls so that Taylor was between him and the short white man.

The white man turned swiftly and disappeared through the door to the cabaret, Sheedy after him. Then Borg came out past Gilroy and clubbed his gun, tapped Taylor back of the ear. Taylor went limp and Kells let him slide down awkwardly to the floor.

Gilroy said: "Well, fo' goodness' sake!"

*   *   *   *   *

They turned off Whittier Boulevard and drove a long way along a well-paved road. The road ran between fields; there were a few dark houses and occasionally a light at an intersection.

Kells sat on the left side of the tonneau and Borg sat on the right side and Taylor was between them. Gilroy and Faber were in front. Gilroy had insisted on coming. Beery had gone home.

Kells said: "Where is Rose?"

Taylor made a resigned gesture with one hand. "I tell you, Mister Kells—I don' know," he said. "If I knew—"

Borg swung his fist around into Taylor's face.

Taylor whimpered and put his arms up over his face. He tried to slide farther down in the seat, and Borg put his arm around his shoulders and held him erect.

"Where's Rose?" Kells pursued relentlessly.

"I don' know, Mister Kells. . . . I swear to God I don' know. . . ." Taylor spoke into the cloth of his coat sleeve; the words were broken, sounded far away.

Borg pulled Taylor's arm down from his face very gently, held his two hands in his lap with one of his hands, swung his fist again.

Taylor struggled and freed one of his hands and put it over his bloody face. "I tell you I got orders that was supposed to come from Rose," he panted—"but they were over the phone . . . I don't know where they was from. . . ."

They rode in silence for a little while, except for the sound of Taylor's sobbing breath. Then they turned into a dirt road, darker, winding.

Kells said: "Where's Rose?"

Taylor sobbed, mumbled unintelligibly.

Gilroy turned around and looked at Taylor with hurt, softly animal eyes. Then he looked at Kells, and Kells nodded. There was a little light from a covered globe on the dashboard. Gilroy kept looking at Kells until he nodded again and then Gilroy tapped Faber's arm; the car stopped, the headlights were switched off.

Kells took the big automatic out of a shoulder holster. He opened the door and put one foot out on the running board, and then he spoke over his shoulder to Borg: "Bring him out here. We don't want to mess up the car."

Taylor screamed and Borg clapped his hand over his mouth—then Taylor was suddenly silent, limp. His eyes were wide and white and his lips moved.

Borg said, "Come on—come on," and then he saw that Taylor couldn't move and he put his arms around him and half shoved, half lifted him out of the door of the car. Taylor couldn't straighten his legs. He put one foot on the running board and his knees gave away and he fell down in the road.

Gilroy got out on the other side, said: "Ah'm goin' to walk up the road a piece." His voice trembled. He went into the darkness.

Taylor was moaning, threshing around in the dust.

Kells squatted beside him. Then he straightened up and spoke to Faber: "Pull up about thirty feet."

Faber looked surprised. He let the clutch in and the car moved forward a little way.

Kells squatted beside Taylor in the darkness again, waited. He held the automatic in his two hands, between his legs. The dim red glow of the taillight was around them.

Taylor rolled over on his back and tried to sit up. Kells helped him, held one hand on his shoulder. Taylor's eyes were bulging; he looked blindly at the redness of the taillight, blindly at Kells—then he said very evenly, quietly: "He's in Pedro—Keystone Hotel. . . ." Fear had worn itself out, had taken his strength and left him, curiously, entirely calm. He no longer trembled and his voice was even, low. Only his eyes were wide, staring.

Kells called to Borg and they helped Taylor back to the car. They picked up Gilroy a little way ahead. He stared questioningly at Taylor, Kells.

Kells said: "He's all right."

They headed back toward town.

* * * * *

The night clerk at the Keystone in San Pedro remembered the gentlemen: the dark, good-looking Mister Gorman and the small and Latin Mister Ribera. They had checked in early yesterday morning, without baggage. They had made several long-distance calls to Los Angeles during the day, sent several wires. They had left about seven-thirty in the evening; no forwarding address.

It was a quarter after one. Kells checked his watch with the clock in the lobby, thanked the clerk and went out to the car. He got in and sat beside Borg, grunted: "No luck."

They had taken Gilroy home—Faber had stayed with him.

Borg asked: "Where to?"

Kells sat a little while silently staring at nothing. He finally said: "Drive down toward Long Beach."

Borg started the car and they went down the dark street

slowly. The fog was very thick; street lights were vague yellow blobs in the darkness.

Kells tapped Borg's knee suddenly. "Have you ever been out to Fay's boat?"

Borg hadn't. "I ain't much of a gambler," he said. "I went out to the *Joanna D.* once, before it burned up—with a broad."

"Do you remember how to get to the P & O wharf?"

Borg said he thought so. They turned into the main highway south. After about a half-hour, they turned off into what turned out to be a blind street. They tried the next one and had just about decided they were wrong again when Borg saw the big white P & O on the warehouse that ran out on the wharf. They parked the car and walked out to the waiting room.

Kells asked the man in the office if the big red-faced man who ran one of the launches to the *Eaglet* was around.

The man looked at his watch. "You mean Bernie, I guess," he said. "He oughta be on his way back with a load."

They sat down and waited.

* * * * *

Bernie laughed. He said: "You ain't as wet as you were the last time I saw you."

Kells shook his head. They walked together to the end of the wharf.

Kells asked: "You know Jack Rose when you see him?"

"Sure."

"When did you see him last?"

Bernie tipped his cap back, scratched his nose. "Night before last," he said, "when you and him went out to the *Joanna.*"

"If you were wanted for murder in L A and wanted to get out of the country for a while how would you do it?"

"I don't know." Bernie spat into the black water alongside the wharf. "I suppose I'd make a pass at Mexico."

"If you were going by car you wouldn't be coming through Pedro."

"No."

"But if you were going by boat? . . ."

Bernie said: "Hell, if I was going by boat I wouldn't go all the way to Mexico. I'd go out and dig in on China Point."

Kells sat down on a pile. "I've heard of it," he said. "What's it all about?"

"That's God's country." Bernie grinned, stared through the sheets of mist at the lights of the bay. "That's the rum runners' paradise. All the boys in the racket along the coast hang out there. They come in from mother ships—and the tender crews. . . . I'll bet there's a million dollars' worth of stuff on the island. They steal it from each other to keep themselves entertained. . . ."

"How long since you were there?"

"Couple years—but I hear about it. They got a swell knock-down drag-out café there now—the Red Barn."

Kells said: "It isn't outside federal jurisdiction."

"No. A cutter goes out and circles the island every month or so. But they pay off plenty—nobody ever bothers 'em."

"That's very interesting," Kells stood up. "How would Rose get out there?"

Bernie shook his head. "A dozen ways. He'd probably get one of the boys who used to run players to the *Joanna* to take him out. It's a two-hour trip in a fast boat."

They walked back toward the waiting room.

Kells said: "It's an awfully long chance. Do you suppose you could get a line on it from any of your friends?"

"I don't think so. I know a couple fellas who worked for Rose and Haardt, but with Rose wanted they wouldn't open up."

Bernie took out a knife and a plug of tobacco, whittled himself a fresh chew.

Kells said: "Try."

"Okay."

They went into the waiting room and Bernie went into the telephone booth.

Borg had found a funny paper. He looked up at Kells, said, "I'll bet the guys that get up these things make a pile of jack—huh?"

Kells said they probably did.

Borg sighed. "I always wanted to be a cartoonist," he said.

Bernie came out of the booth in a little while. "There's a man named Carver got a string of U Drive pleasure boats down at Long Beach," he said. "He says a couple men and a woman hired one about eight-thirty and ain't come back

95

yet. One of 'em sounds like Rose. The other was a little guy; and the woman, he don't know about—she was bundled up."

Kells smiled as if he meant it, said: "Come on."

"We wouldn't get out there till daylight in my boat. Maybe I can borrow the *Comet*—I'll go see."

Bernie went out, came back in a few minutes shaking his head.

"He wants fifty dollars till ten in the morning," he said. "That's too damn much."

Kells took a sheaf of bills out of his pocket, peeled off two.

"Give him whatever he wants out of this," he said. "And does he want a deposit?"

"No." Bernie started for the door. "He keeps my boat for security."

Kells and Borg followed him out, across the wharf, across a rickety foot bridge and down to a wide float.

Bernie gave the man who was waiting there one of the bills, said: "I'll pick up the change when I come back."

The man asked: "Don't you want me to come along?"

Bernie glanced at Kells.

Kells said: "Thanks—no. We'll get along."

The *Comet* was a trim thirty-foot craft; mahogany and steel and glistening brass. She looked very fast.

Bernie switched on the running lights and started the engine. The man cast off the lines; Bernie spun the wheel over and they swung in a wide curve away from the float and out through the narrows to the cut that led to the outer bay.

The fog was broken to long trailing shreds. The swell was long, fairly easy.

Bernie snapped on the binnacle light. "I hope I ain't forgot the course," he said. "I think it'll clear up when we get out a ways—but I'm usually wrong about fog."

Borg said, "That's dandy," with dripping sarcasm.

Kells went down into the little cabin, lay down on one of the bunks and watched the red and green and yellow buoy lights slide swiftly by the portholes. After a while they rounded the breakwater and there weren't any more lights to watch.

Kells was awakened by Bernie whispering: "We made it in an hour and fifty minutes." Then Bernie went outside.

It was very dark. Borg was lying in the other bunk, groaning faintly.

Kells said: "What the hell's the matter?"

Borg didn't answer.

"You aren't sick!" Kells was emphatically incredulous.

It was quiet for a minute and then Borg said slowly: "Who's the best judge of that—me or you?"

Kells got up and went outside. Bernie had doused the running lights; there was a thin glow from the binnacle—and darkness. The fog felt like a wet sheet.

Bernie said: "There's a big cruiser tied up on the other wharf. I coasted by close—I don't think there's anybody aboard."

"Any other boats?"

"I couldn't see any." Bernie switched off the binnacle light. "There's another little cove on the other side of the island, but nobody uses it."

Kells said: "We're not tied up, are we?"

"Sure."

Kells looked at Bernie admiringly. "You're a wonder. It didn't even wake me up."

Bernie chuckled. "You're damn right I'm a wonder."

They climbed up on the wharf, crossed quietly. The cruiser was big, luxurious, evidently deserted—Bernie couldn't make out the name. Except for a few rowboats and the *Comet*, it was the only boat at the wharf.

Kells said: "Well—I guess I'm wrong again."

They walked up the wharf, and Bernie found a path and they walked along the bottom of a shallow gully, up to the left across a kind of ridge.

The fog was so heavy they didn't see the light until they were about twenty feet from it. Then they went forward silently and a big ramshackle shed took form in the gray darkness. The light came from a square window on the second floor.

Bernie said: "This used to be a cattle shelter—they've built onto it. I guess it's the place they call the Red Barn."

They found a door and Kells knocked twice. There was

no answer, so he turned the knob, pushed the door open.

There was a kerosene lamp at one end of a short bar. The room was long, windowless; the ceiling sloped to a high peak at one end. There was a stairway leading up to a balcony of rough timbers, and there was an open door on the balcony leading into a lighted room.

At first Kells thought the downstairs room was deserted; then by the flickering uncertain light of the lamp he saw a man asleep at one of the half dozen or so tables. There was another man lying on a cot against one wall. He rolled over and said, "Wha'd' you want?" sleepily. Kells didn't answer—the man looked at him blearily for a moment and then grunted and rolled back with his face to the wall.

A man came out on the balcony and stood with his hands on the railing, silently staring down at them. He was of medium height, appeared in the inadequate light to be dark, swarthy.

Kells said: "How are chances of buying a drink?"

The man suddenly stepped out of the doorway so that a little more light fell on Kells' upturned face. Then he threw back his head and laughed noiselessly. His shoulders shook and his face was twisted with mirth, but there was no sound.

Bernie looked at Kells. Kells turned and glanced at the man on the cot, looked up at the swarthy man again. The man stopped laughing, looked down and spoke in a hoarse whisper:

"Sure. Come up."

He turned, disappeared into the room.

Kells said, "Wait," to Bernie. He went up the stairs two at a time, into the room.

It was a fairly large room, square. There were a few rather good rugs on the floor, a flat-topped desk near the far wall, several chairs. There were two big lamps—the kind that have to be pumped up, hiss when lighted.

The man closed the door behind him, went to the desk and sat down. He waved his hand at a chair but Kells shook his head slightly, stood still.

The man's face was familiar. It was deeply lined and the eyes were very far apart, very dark. His mouth was full and red, and his hair was very short, black.

Kells asked: "Where do I remember you from?"

The man shook his head. "You don't." There was some sort of curious impediment in his speech. Then he smiled. "I'm Crotti."

Kells pulled a chair closer to the desk. He said: "I'll still buy a drink."

Crotti opened a drawer and took out a squat square bottle, a glass. He pushed them across the desk, said: "Help yourself."

Kells poured himself a drink, sat down.

He knew Crotti very well by reputation, had once had him pointed out in a theater crowd in New York. A big-timer, he had started as a minor gangster in Detroit, become in the space of three or four years a national figure. A flair for color, a certain genius for organization, good political connections had kept him alive, out of jail and at the top. The press had boomed him as a symbol: the Crime Magnate—in New York he was supposed to be the power behind the dope ring, organized prostitution and gambling, the beer business—everything that was good for copy.

Crotti said: "This is a miracle." His voice was very thin, throaty.

Kells remembered that he had heard something of an operation affecting the vocal cords, that Crotti always spoke in this curious confidential manner.

He asked: "What's a miracle?"

Crotti leaned back in his chair. "In the morning," he said, "your hotel was to be called, an invitation was to be extended to you to visit me—out here."

He opened a box of cigars on the desk, offered them to Kells, carefully selected one.

"And here you are."

Kells didn't answer.

Crotti clipped and lighted his cigar, leaned back again. "What do you think of that?"

Kells said: "What do you want?"

"Since you anticipated my invitation may I ask what *you* want?"

Kells sipped his drink, shrugged. "I came out for a drink of good whiskey," he said.

He looked around the room. There were two closed doors

on his right, a window on his left. In front of him, behind Crotti, there was another large square window—the one he had seen from the outside. He finished his drink, put the glass on the desk.

"I'm looking for a fella named Jack Rose," he said. "Ever hear of him?"

Crotti nodded.

"Know where he is?"

"No." Crotti smiled, shook his head.

They were both silent for a minute. Crotti puffed comfortably at his cigar and Kells waited.

Crotti cleared his throat finally, said: "You've done very well."

Kells waited.

"You've helped eliminate a lot of small fry: Haardt, Perry, O'Donnell—you've run Rose out of town and you have the Fenner and Bellmann factions pretty well in hand. You can write your own ticket . . ."

"You make it sound swell." Kells poured himself a drink. "What about it?"

"I'm going to cut you in."

Kells widened his eyes extravagantly. "What do you mean—cut me in?"

"I'm going to clean up all the loose ends and turn the whole business over to you . . ."

Kells said: "My, my—isn't that dandy!" He put the full glass down on the desk. "What the hell are you talking about?"

Crotti flicked the ashes from his cigar, leaned forward.

"Listen," he said. "Things are pretty hot back East. I've been running a couple ships up here with stuff from Mexico for a year. Now, I'm going to move *all* my interests here, the whole layout. I'm going to take over the coast."

"And? . . ."

"And you're in."

Kells said: "I'm out."

Crotti leaned back again, studied the gray tip of his cigar. He smiled slowly. "I think you're in," he said.

* * * * *

Kells took a little tin box of aspirin out of his pocket, put two tablets on his tongue and washed them down with whiskey.

100

"You seem to have kept pretty well in touch with things out here."

Crotti said: "Yes. I sent an operative out a few weeks ago to look things over—a very clever girl. . . ." He took the cigar out of his mouth. "Name's Granquist."

Kells sat very still. He looked at Crotti and then he grinned slowly, broadly.

Crotti grinned back. "Am I right in assuming that you were looking for Rose because you thought he had something to do with Miss Granquist's—uh—escape?"

Kells didn't answer.

Crotti stood up. "I always take care of my people," he said as pompously as his squeaky voice would permit. He went to one of the doors, swung it open. The inner room was dark.

Crotti called: "Hey—Swede."

There was no answer. Crotti went into the room; Kells could hear him whispering, evidently trying to wake someone up.

He unbuttoned his coat, shifted the shoulder holster. Crotti reappeared in the doorway, and Granquist was behind him. Crotti went back to his chair, sat down.

Granquist stood in the doorway, swaying. Her eyes were heavy with sleep and she stared drunkenly about the room, finally focused on Kells. She sneered as if it were difficult for her to control her facial muscles, put one hand on the doorframe to steady herself.

She said thickly: "Hello—bastard."

Kells looked away from her, spoke to Crotti. "Nice quiet girl. Just the kind you want to take home and introduce to your folks."

Crotti laughed soundlessly.

Granquist staggered forward, stood swaying above Kells. "Bastard framed me," she mumbled—"tried t' tag me f' murder. . . ."

She put one hand out tentatively as if she were about to catch a fly, slapped Kells very hard across the face.

Crotti stood up suddenly.

Kells reached out and pushed Granquist away gently, said: "Don't be effeminate."

Crotti came around the desk and took Granquist by the

shoulders, pressed her down into a chair. She was swearing brokenly, incoherently; she put her hands up to her face, sobbed.

Crotti said: "Be quiet." He turned to Kells with a deprecating smile. "I'm sorry."

Kells didn't say anything.

It was quiet for a little while except for Granquist's strangled, occasional sobs. Crotti sat down on the edge of the desk.

Kells was staring thoughtfully at Granquist. Finally he turned to Crotti, said: "I played the Bellmann business against this one"—he jerked his head at Granquist—"because it was good sense, and because I knew I could clear her if it got warm. Then when she got away I figured Rose had her and went into the panic. I've been leaping all over Southern California with a big hero act while she's been sitting on her lead over here with an armful of bottles. . . ."

He sighed, shook his head. "When I'm right, I'm wrong."

Then he went on as if thinking aloud: "Rose and Abalos and a woman—probably Rose's wife—hired a boat at Long Beach tonight and didn't come back."

Crotti glanced at Granquist. "Rose had an interest in one of the big booze boats," he said—"the *Santa Maria*. She was lying about sixty miles off the coast a couple days ago. He probably headed out there."

He puffed hard at his cigar, put it down on an ashtray, leaned forward.

"Now about my proposition . . ." he said. "You've started a good thing but you can't finish it by yourself. I've got the finest organization in the country and I'm going to put it at your disposal so that you can do this thing the way it should be done—to the limit. LA county is big enough for everybody—"

Kells interrupted: "I think I've heard that someplace before."

Crotti paid no attention to the interruption, went on: "—for everybody—but things have got to be under a single head. This thing of everybody cutting everybody else's throat is bad business—small-town stuff."

Kells nodded very seriously.

"We can have things working like a charm in a couple weeks if we go at it right," Crotti went on excitedly. "Organization is the thing. We'll organize gambling, the bootleggers, the city and state and federal police—*everything.*"

He stood up, his eyes glittering with enthusiasm. "We can jerk five million dollars a year out of this territory—*five million dollars.*"

Kells whistled.

Granquist had put her hands down. She was sitting deep in the chair, glaring at Kells. Crotti picked up his cigar and walked up and down, puffing out great clouds of blue-gray smoke.

"Why, right this minute," he said, "I've got a hundred and fifteen thousand dollars' worth of French crystal cocaine on one of my boats—a hundred and fifteen thousand dollars' worth, wholesale. All it needs is protected landing and distribution to a dozen organized dealers."

Kells nodded, pouring himself another drink.

Crotti sat down at the desk, took out a handkerchief and wiped his face.

"And you're the man for it," he said. "My money's on you. . . ."

Kells said, "That's fine," smiled appreciatively.

"Your split is twenty per cent of everything." Crotti crushed his cigar out, leaned back and regarded Kells benignly. "Everything—the whole take."

Kells was watching Crotti. He moved his eyes without moving his head, looked at Granquist. "That ought to pay for a lot of telephone calls," he said.

"Then it's a deal."

"No."

Crotti looked as if he'd found a cockroach in his soup. He said incredulously: "You mean it isn't enough?"

"Too much."

"Then why not?"

Kells said: "Because I don't like it. Because I never worked for anybody in my life and I'm too old to start. Because I don't like the racket, anyway—I was aced in. It's full of tinhorns and two-bit politicians and double-crossers—the whole damned business gives me a severe pain in the backside." He paused, glanced at Granquist.

"Rose and Fenner both tried to frame me," he went on. "That made me mad and I fought back. I was lucky—I took advantage of a couple breaks and got myself into a spot where I could have some fun."

He stood up. "Now you want to spoil my fun."

Crotti stood up, too. He shook his head. "No," he said. "I want to show you how to make it pay."

Kells said: "I'm sorry. It's a swell proposition but I'm not the man for it—I guess I'm not commercially inclined. It's not my game. . . ."

Crotti shrugged elaborately. "All right."

Kells said: "Now, if you'll ask the man behind me to put his rod away I'll be going."

Crotti's lips were pressed close together, curved up at the corners. He turned and looked into the big window behind him—the man who stood just inside the doorway through which they had entered was reflected against outer darkness.

Crotti nodded to the man and at the same moment Granquist stood up, screamed. Kells stepped into line between Crotti and the door, whirled in the same second—the big automatic was in his hand, belching flame.

The man had evidently been afraid of hitting Crotti, was two slugs late. He looked immensely surprised, crashed down sideways in the doorway. Crotti was standing with his back to the window, the same curved grimace on his face.

There were pounding steps on the stair. Kells stepped over the man in the doorway, ran smack into another—the man who had been asleep on the cot—at the top of the stair. The man grabbed him around the waist before he could use the gun; he raised it, felt the barrel-sight rip across the man's face. There were several more men in the big room below, two on the stairs, coming up.

He planted one foot in the angle of the floor and wall, shoved hard; locked together, they balanced precariously for a moment, fell. They hit the two men about halfway down, tangled to a twisted mass of threshing arms, legs. The banister creaked, gave way. Kells felt the collar of his coat grabbed, was jerked under and down. He struck out with the gun, squeezed it. The gun roared and he heard

104

someone yell and then something hit the center of his forehead and there was darkness.

The fog was wet on Kells' face. He opened his eyes and
looked up into the grayness, rolled over on his side
slowly, looked into thick, unbroken grayness. He held his
hand in front of him at arm's length and it was a shapeless
mass of darker gray. He sat up and leaden weights fell in
his skull like the mechanism that opens and closes the eyes
of dolls. He lay down again and turned his head slowly,
held his watch close. It was a little after six, full daylight,
but the fog made it night.

Then he heard someone coming, the crunch of feet on
gravel. He reached for the gun, found the empty holster,
noticed suddenly with a sharp sensation in the pit of his
stomach that his coat was gone.

Someone squatted beside him, spoke: "How d' you
feel?" It was Borg. Kells could see the thick outline of his
head and shoulders.

Kells said: "Terrible. Where the hell's my coat?"

"God! Me saving his life an' he wants his coat!" Borg giggled softly.

"What happened?"

"Everything." Borg sighed, sat down in the gravel with
his mouth close to Kells' ear. "After you an' the navigator
went ashore I went on the wharf and laid down for a while.
Then in a couple minutes somebody came out an' I thought
it was you till I seen there was four of them. I ducked
behind some ropes and stuff that was laying there and they
came out and saw the boat an' jawed awhile in some spick
language. Then they lit out for some place an' I got up and
tailed them and run into the navigator."

There was the sound of a shot suddenly, some place
below and to Kells' left.

Borg said: "That's him now—what a boy!"

Kells sat up.

Borg went on: "He was carrying on about smelling

trouble up at some kind of barn an' he wanted a gun. I wouldn't give him mine, so he said he was going back to the boat an' bust open a locker or something where he thought there was one. He—"

There was another shot.

Kells said: "What the hell's *that* all about?" He jerked his head toward the sound, immediately wished he hadn't.

"That's him—he's all right. Wait'll I tell you. . . ." Borg shifted his position a little, went on: "I went on up the path an' I'll be damned if that navigator didn't catch up with me, an' he had the dirtiest-looking shotgun I ever saw. When we got to the house, he said, 'You go in the front way an' I'll go in the back,' so I waited for him to get around to the back—an' about that time there was two shots inside."

Kells lay down again on his stomach. Borg twisted around, lay beside him.

"I went in and you was doing a cartwheel downstairs with three or four guys on your neck. There was another guy there an' he made a pass at me and I shot him right between the eyes. . . ."

Borg leaned close to Kells, tapped his own head between the eyes with a stubby forefinger.

Kells said: "Hurry up."

"I'm hurrying. They was tearing hell out of you an' I was trying to pick one of 'em off when the navigator came in the back way and started waving that shotgun around. He yelled so much they *had* to see him. Then another guy came out on the balcony and I took a shot at him, but I guess I missed—he ducked back in the upstairs room."

Borg sighed, shook his head. There was another shot below, then two more, close together.

"Well—I got off to one side to give the navigator a chance," Borg went on, "but he had a better idea—he came over on my side and we jockeyed around till I could get a hold of you, and then we backed out the front—me dragging you, and the navigator telling the boys what a swell lot of hash they'd make if he let go with that meat grinder. When we got outside I drug you a little to one side—"

Kells interrupted: "Didn't I have my coat?"

"Hell, no! You was lucky to have pants the way those guys was working you over. We tried to carry you between us but we couldn't make any headway that way—it was so dark and foggy we kept falling down. So the navigator fanned tail for the boat and I drug you through a lot of brush and we got up here after a while. A half a dozen more guys went by on the way to the house—the island's lousy with 'em. If it hadn't been for the fog . . ."

Kells asked: "Bernie's at the boat, now?"

"Sure—and a swell spot. The fog's not quite so heavy down there and he can pick 'em off as soon as they show at the head of the wharf. Only I thought he'd shove off before this. . . ."

"He's waiting for us, sap." Kells rose to his knees.

"Oh yeah? Maybe *you* can figure out a way for us to get there."

Kells asked: "Which direction should the side of the cove be?"

"I haven't the slightest."

Kells got shakily to his feet, rubbed his head, started down a shale bank to his left. He said: "Come on—we'll have to take a chance."

Borg got up and they went down the bank to a shallow draw. An occasional shot sounded on the far side of a low ridge to their right. The fog wasn't quite so thick at the bottom of the draw; they went on, came out in a little while onto a narrow beach. There was a jagged spit of rock running out across the sand from one side of the draw. The fog was thinning.

They waited for the next shot; then Kells, calculating direction from the sound, said, "Come on"—they ran out along the rocks to the edge of the water.

Kells kicked off his shoes, waded in; Borg followed. The fog was heavy over the water—they swam blindly in the direction Kells figured the *Comet* to be.

After a little while the end of the wharf took form ahead, a bit to the right. They circled toward it, came up to the bow of the big cruiser. They swam around the cruiser, under the wharf and up to the *Comet*'s stern.

Kells grabbed the gunwale, pulled himself up a little way and called to Bernie. Bernie was crouched in the forward end of the cockpit, behind the raised forward deck. He whirled and swung the gun toward Kells, and then he grinned broadly, put down the gun, crawled over and helped Kells climb aboard. He muttered, "Good huntin'," went back and picked up the gun; Kells helped Borg.

Borg was winded—he lay at full length on the deck, gasping for breath. Kells started toward Bernie, and then his bad leg gave way, he fell down, crawled the rest of the way.

He said: "Get the engine started—I'll take that for a minute."

Bernie gave him the gun and a handful of shells, went down to the engine. Kells called to Borg, told him to work his way to the after line, cut it. There was a shot at the head of the wharf, a piece of wood was torn from the edge of the cowling, fell in splinters.

Borg rolled over slowly, got to his knees. He was still panting. He looked reproachfully at Kells, fumbled in his pocket and took out a small jackknife, started worming his way aft.

The engine went over with a roar.

There was an answering roar of shots from the shore.

Bernie came galloping up to the wheel. Kells glanced back at Borg, saw him sawing at the stern line; he took a bead on the bow line, pulled the trigger. The line frayed; Kells aimed again, gave it the other barrel.

Bernie said: "That's enough—I can part it now. . . ." He slid the clutch in, threw the wheel over.

Kells was hastily reloading. He glanced back at Borg, saw the stern line fall, saw Borg sink down exhausted, so flat that he was safe.

The bow line snapped. They skipped in a fast shallow arc toward the head of the wharf. There was a rattle of gunfire. Kells pushed the shotgun across the cowling, sighted. Two puffs of smoke grew over an overturned dinghy on the beach; he swung the barrel toward the smoke, pulled the trigger.

Then they straightened out, headed through the mouth of the cove toward the open sea. Bernie kicked the throttle. A few desultory shots popped behind them.

Kells put down the gun, sat down on the deck and rolled up his wet trouser leg. The leg wasn't very nice to look at— Doc Janis's dressing was hanging by a thin strip of adhesive tape. Kells called Borg.

Borg got up slowly. He came forward, squatted beside Kells.

Bernie yelled: "There's some peroxide and stuff in the for'd locker on the port side—I busted it open."

Borg went into the cabin.

Kells fished in his trouser pockets, brought out a wad of wet bills and some silver, spread it out on the deck beside him. There was a thousand-dollar note and the eight hundreds which Brand's friend had paid off with after the fights. There was another wad of fifty- and hundred-dollar and smaller bills. Fenner's twenty-five-thousand-dollar check, Brand's for a thousand, and around eight thousand in cash had been in the coat. And Fenner's confession.

Kells looked up; Bernie was looking at him, grinned. "Wet as usual," he said. "You better take off your clothes an' get in a bunk."

Kells said: "Step on it. I've got to call up a friend of mine."

He picked up several of the wet bills, folded them, put a half dollar inside the fold to give them weight, slid them across the deck to Bernie.

"That ought to cover damages on the boat, too," he said.

Borg came out of the cabin with absorbent cotton and adhesive and peroxide.

Kells picked up some more bills, rolled them into a ball and shoved them into Borg's free hand, said: "Try to buy yourself a yacht with that . . ."

He counted what was left.

Borg poured peroxide on the leg.

Kells said: "I came out to California with two grand." He shoved the bills into a heap. There was a little pile of silver left. He counted it with his finger.

"Now I've got two—and seventy cents." He picked up the silver, held it in his palm, smiled at Borg.

"Velvet."

Bernie shouted: "I hope I remember the way back!"

Kells said: "Don't let that worry you," stared forward into the fog.

* * * * *

There was a small zebra galloping up and down the footboard. He was striped red white blue like a barber pole; his ears were tasseled, flopped back and forth awkwardly. Then he faded into a bright mist; the room tipped over to darkness. Kells yelled . . .

Then it was raining outside. Gray. . . .

After a while Kells opened his eyes and looked up at Borg, said: "Hello, baby," softly.

Borg giggled. He said: "Don't be sentimental."

Doc Janis came over and stared bleakly down over Borg's shoulder. He said: "By God! I never saw such a tough egg."

Kells blinked at him, closed his eyes. He heard Janis talking to Borg as if from a great distance: "Give him all the whiskey he wants, but no more of *this*. Understand?"

Kells wondered idly what *this* was. He mumbled, "Gimme drink a water," fell asleep.

When he awoke he lay with his eyes closed listening to rain beat against the windows.

He said, "What time is it?" opened his eyes.

Borg and Shep Beery were playing cards on a table in the center of the room. Beery said: "That's twice I've ruined my hand waiting for three hundred pinochle." He got up and came over to the bed, grinned down at Kells.

"What do you care—you're not going any place."

Kells looked past Beery at Borg, looked around the room. He said: "What the hell is this?"

Borg was shuffling the cards. There was a bridge lamp beside the table and the light fell squarely on his fat, pale face. He shook his head sadly without looking up.

"Slug-nutty."

Beery sat down on the edge of the bed, whispered confidentially: "This is the Palace, Gerry—you're the Prince of Wales. . . ."

"I'm Mary, Queen of Snots." Borg looked up, smiled complacently.

Kells closed his eyes, said: "Give me a drink."

Beery reached over and took a tumbler, a big bottle from a stand beside the bed, poured a drink; Kells sat up slowly, carefully.

Beery handed him the glass. "You've been out like a light for a few days. We didn't figure the hotel was a good spot right now so we moved you over here. It's the Miramar, on Franklin."

110

Kells held the glass with both shaking hands, tipped it, drank deeply.

Borg got up, came over and leaned on the foot of the bed. "Where do you remember to?" he asked.

Kells handed the empty glass to Beery, lay down. "When we got back from the island, I phoned Fenner—and had Bernie get a bottle. . . ."

"*Four* bottles. . . . And you sucked up three of 'em. I had to practically clip you to get a swallow. You said your leg hurt an' you wanted to get drunk. . . ."

Kells said: "Sure, I remember. . . ."

"You did."

Beery chuckled. "Uh huh," he said. "You did."

"Then when we got you to the hotel," Borg went on, "an' into bed, you started having the screaming heebies and the Doc give you a shot in the arm—so you got worse. . . ."

Kells smiled faintly. His eyes were closed.

"The Doc was running around in circles wringing his hands because he thought the leg was going to gangrene or something. You started roaring for more M, and then when I left you alone for a minute you got up an' promoted a tube of hyoscine someplace, an' a needle . . ." Borg paused, straightening up and finished disgustedly: "An' I'll be goddamned if you didn't shoot the whole bloody tube!"

Beery said: "Then you began to get really violent—tried to do a hundred an' eighty out the window, wanted to walk across the ceiling—things like that. We smuggled you out of the hotel and brought you over here."

Kells said: "Give me a drink, Shep."

He sat up again slowly, took the glass. "How many days?"

Beery said: "Four."

Kells drank, laughed. "Four bottles—four days. . . . Four's my lucky number . . ." He squinted at Borg. "Once I bet four yards on a four-to-one shot in the fourth race on the Fourth of July . . ." He handed the glass to Beery, sank back on the pillow. "Horse ran fourth."

Borg snorted, turned and went into the bathroom. Kells looked around the room again. "Nice joint," he said. "How much am I paying for it?"

"I don't know." Beery lighted a cigaret. "Fenner has

some kind of lien or mortgage or something on the building—he said he'd take care of the details."

"It was his suggestion—bringing me here?"

Beery nodded.

"Where is he?"

"Long gone. When you told him Crotti had his confession he scrammed. I got him on the phone just before he checked out of the Knickerbocker and he said he'd call over here and fix it for the apartment—said he'd get in touch with you later."

Kells smiled. "All the big boys . . . It's simply a process of elimination. Fenner and Rose gone—Bellmann dead. Now if we can only angle Crotti into committing suicide . . ." He paused, glanced at Borg coming back from the bath. "Did Fat, here, tell you all about the island sequence?"

Borg said: "Sure I told him—all I knew."

"Crotti propositioned me to come in with him on a big play to organize the whole coast," Kells went on. "Will you please tell me why these bastards keep dealing me in, and then figure that if I'm not for 'em I'm against 'em? First Rose—but that was an out-and-out frame; then Fenner thought *he* and I'd make a great team. Now, Crotti—and the funny part of that one is I think he was on the level about it."

Beery said: "It must be the way you wear your clothes."

"Sure. It's just your natural charm." Borg made a wry face, went back to the table and began laying out solitaire.

"Of course Crotti's got the right idea about organization." Kells rubbed his eyes with his knuckles. "But the fun in an organization is being head man."

Beery said: "The other night at Fenner's when you were putting on that act for Gowdy, you said you had some friends on the way out here. Was that a gag?"

"Certainly. I wanted to impress Gowdy with my importance to his outfit. You can get my torpedo friends in the East into a telephone booth."

"Well—if Crotti says war"—Beery got up and went over to one of the rain-swept windows—"we're sitting pretty. . . ."

"Uh huh." Borg looked at Kells. "In a pig's eye. We three, an' whatever strong-arm strength Gowdy swings—and that doesn't amount to a hell of a lot. . . ."

"And against us. . . ." Beery turned from the window, stuck his hands deep in his pockets. "There's all Crotti's mob—and that's supposed to be the best in the country. There's Rose, with his syndicate behind him, and all the loogans he's imported from back East. There's the Bellmann outfit. They weren't very efficient when they blew up the print shop the other day, but you can't figure from that—"

"And by God!—most of *them* are in uniform," Borg interrupted.

Beery smiled faintly, nodded. "Uh huh—we're in a swell spot."

Kells was staring at the ceiling. He said: "Now's a good time to get out."

Beery looked at Borg; Borg took a toothpick out of his vest pocket, stuck it in his mouth and went back to his solitaire.

"I didn't mean that," Beery said. "Only, what are we going to do?"

"Get out." Kells' eyes were fixed blankly on the ceiling. "I've been pretty lucky up to now. Partly because everybody that's been against me has figured that the inside would get a big press spread if anything serious happened to me."

He looked at Beery. "Through you—spread through you, I mean. That doesn't make it very safe for you."

Beery was looking at the floor.

"The luck's beginning to run out," Kells went on. "I dropped all the dough I'd made since I've been out here, on the island, because I was dumb enough to get heroic about that bitch Granquist—and she was Crotti's plant all the time. . . ."

Beery said: "You didn't tell me about that."

"I'm telling you now. She was sent out here by Crotti to look things over—start the organization ball rolling."

"Well well. Damned clever, these Swedes." Beery sat down at the table.

No one said anything for a minute. Beery watched Borg play solitaire. Kells' eyes wandered again to the ceiling.

"You're absolutely right," he finally said. "We'd better take a sneak while we're all in one piece."

Beery stood up and poured himself a drink. He waved

113

the glass at Kells. He said: "We've gone too far—an' it's too much fun. We can still smack the Bellmann administration down—and anyway, these rats don't know whether we're strong or not. You'll be up and around in a couple days—we can count on a hand from Fay, if we need it. . . ."

Borg was staring at the cards. He said, "Sure," without looking up.

"No." Kells shook his head slowly. "It's too tough. You boys have been a great help, but—"

"Shut up! You can crawl out if you want to, but I'll stick—I'm having a swell time." Beery grinned down at Kells, gulped his drink.

Borg looked up, said, "Sure," quietly. He stood up.

Kells laughed. He glanced at the bottle on the bedstand, said: "Draw three, Shep."

* * * * *

They had dinner sent up from Musso-Frank's, on the Boulevard.

Doctor Janis stopped by about nine o'clock.

"Two days," he said—"two more days at least. Then you can go out for a little while, if you take it easy—on crutches."

Kells was sweating; his eyes burned and he yawned a great deal. He said: "Maybe I'd better have one more load in the arm, Doc—to sort of taper off on."

"You'll taper off on whiskey and milk, young fella—and like it." The doctor put two small yellow capsules on the stand. "If you get too jumpy you can take these before you go to sleep."

Janis and Beery went out together; Beery was going home. Borg played solitaire for a while and Kells sat up in bed, tried to read the papers.

Borg said: "Denny Faber is still trailing around with Gilroy."

"You can call him off—Gilroy ought to be okay by now."

At eleven Borg stood up, stretched, said: "I'm going byebye." He went into the bedroom—Kells was on the wall bed in the living room. Borg came back in his underwear, got Kells a glass of water, made a pass at tucking him in.

"If you want anything," he said, "just yell and fire a few

shots and throw your shoe through the window. I'm a very light sleeper."

Kells said he would.

Borg went back into the bedroom and Kells turned out the lights, tried to sleep. He heard the bell in the big church on Sunset Boulevard strike twelve. Rain drummed against the windows, and the wind was blowing.

Sometime around one he got up, hobbled into the bath. He scrubbed his teeth and got back to the bed by using a chair for support, hopping slowly on one foot. He took the capsules Janis had left, washed them down with whiskey and water. He slept after a while—heavily, dreamlessly.

When he awoke he lay rigid for a little while listening to rain beating against the windows. Then a voice whispered close to his ear: "Wake up—darling."

Kells lay very still, turned his eyes toward the darkness. Granquist said: "Wake up—darling."

Kells moved his head until he could see the silhouette of her crouched body against the pale reflected light of the wall.

She spoke rapidly, breathlessly: "Are you all right, darling—can you walk? We've got to get out of here right away . . ."

He smiled a little and raised his head a little and said: "Will you please go away? . . ."

She sank to her knees beside the bed and tried to take his head in her arms.

"Please," she said. "We've got to go quickly. Please. . . ."

Kells put her arms away and sat up and pulled the pillows up behind him. "How the hell did you get in?"

"I put on an act for the night man—told him I wanted to surprise you. He came up and let me in with the passkey . . ."

"Go on—surprise me."

"Gerry," Granquist's eyes were big in the faint light; drops of rain glistened on her small dark hat, her dark close-fitting coat—"I've been in an awfully bad spot since you shot up Crotti's camp. I got away this afternoon when Fenner came out to do business about his confession—Crotti didn't know anything about it but he let Fenner think he did . . ."

"What do you mean, Crotti didn't know about it?" Kells put his hand on her wrist.

"I got to your coat first—I've got Fenner's confession and his certified check for twenty-five thou—and your cash. . . ."

She clicked open a small handbag, took out a handful of crumpled papers and currency, dropped it on the bed. He looked down at it a little while and then he let his head fall back again against the pillow, bent it slightly sideways.

He said: "You're a strange gal." He put his hand on her wrist again, held it tightly.

She tried to speak. She got up and walked to the window and then back, sat down on the edge of the bed.

Kells asked: "Why do we have to leave here?"

"Because you haven't Fenner's protection any longer—he thinks Crotti has this"—she nodded at the stuff on the bed. "The whole layout is against you now—Crotti, Rose, Fenner, the Bellmann people. . . ."

Kells switched on the lamp beside the bed, unfolded and smoothed out the sheet of Lido stationery with Fenner's shakily signed confession.

"We have this," he said. "Fenner hasn't played ball—I can stick it into him and break it off. And we've got around thirty-five grand. We're in a swell spot to play both ends against the middle."

"No, Gerry." Her voice was harsh, strained. "Please, no, Gerry—let's go away, quick. I'm scared. . . ."

Kells was silent a while, looking at her abstractedly.

Then he said: "The middle against both ends, by God!"

He put out one arm and cupped his hand against the back of Granquist's neck and pulled her to him.

*   *   *   *   *

In the morning the sun came out warm, bright.

At about nine-thirty Borg came out of the bedroom in trousers and a green silk undershirt. Granquist had had things sent up from the commissary, was preparing breakfast in the kitchen. Borg leaned against the side of the door and looked at her and then he smiled blankly at Kells, said: "Well, well."

"From now on"—Kells bent his head a little to one side—"Fenner's on the other team."

Borg went to the table and sat down. "I still like your side," he said—"an' I want to pitch."

116

"You're not very bright. See if you can get Faber on the phone—tell him to come up here."

Borg reached for the phone, dialed a number.

Granquist brought breakfast in on a big tray. There was orange juice and an omelette and toast and coffee.

Borg finally got Faber and talked to him a little while, and then he looked up Woodward's number in the Dell Building, downtown, dialed it, took the phone to Kells.

Kells said, "Hello," asked for Woodward, and then he said: "This is Kells. If you come out to the Miramar Apartments on Franklin and Cherokee, in Hollywood, I think we might do a little business." He hung up, smiled at Granquist.

"You'll have to duck while he's here, baby," he said. "He's the undercover legal representative for the Bellmann administration and you're still number one suspect for Bellmann's shooting—you'll have to lay low till we hang it on Fenner and make it stick."

She nodded.

After a little while someone knocked at the door; Borg got up and let Beery in. Beery threw his hat on a chair, stared with bright, surprised eyes at Granquist, said: "Well—it's a small world."

She smiled. "Coffee?"

Beery nodded and Granquist went out into the kitchen.

Kells said: "Fenner went out to see Crotti yesterday."

Beery sat down, smiled down his nose.

"Now we don't have to worry about kicking any of our crowd in the tail," Kells went on, "because we haven't got any."

Beery raised his brows, said: "Crowd?"

"Uh huh—crowd."

Beery glanced around the room, back to Kells. "Since this joint was Fenner's suggestion," he said, "wouldn't it be a swell time to move?"

Kells shook his head slowly. "What for? Any of 'em can find me if they want me—and they'll all be wanting to before long. This is as good a spot as any. . . ."

Granquist came in with coffee and toast on a small tray, Beery stood up, bowed, took the tray and sat down.

Kells said: "I'm going to turn on the heat—Shep—only

this time I'm going to make it pay. It's been for fun up to now—now it's for dough."

Borg was playing solitaire at the table. He looked up, said, "Hooray," dryly.

"The lady"—Kells inclined his head toward Granquist—"picked up all the stuff I lost at Crotti's. Fenner thinks Crotti's got his confession, but I've got it—and Fenner's going to find out about that. So is Woodward, who ought to be willing to give his eye teeth—and the mayor's eye teeth—for it. He's on his way up here now."

Beery lighted a cigaret.

"They can both buy it," Kells went on, "and for plenty."

He turned to Borg. "See if you can get Hanline at the Knickerbocker."

Borg picked up the phone, dialed a number. After a moment he got up and handed the phone to Kells.

Kells said: "Hello—Hanline? . . . Tell that boss of yours that I've got the stuff he's dealing with Crotti about. Tell him that in the next two hours I'm going to sell it to the best offer. He'll know what I mean . . . Tell him that the bidding starts at fifty grand, and that he'd better be damned quick. . . ."

Kells hung up, grinned at Beery. "Now watch things happen," he said.

Beery was looking at Granquist. "Where does Miss G get off if you peddle Fenner's confession back to him? It's the one thing that leaves her in the clear."

Kells moved his grin to Granquist. "We've figured that out," he said.

The house-phone rang: Borg answered it, said, "Send him up," hung up. He said, "Faber," over his shoulder, went to the door.

Granquist looked questioningly at Kells.

Kells shook his head. "Borg's running mate—I'll give you twelve guesses where I'm going to send him."

Faber came in, said hello to Kells and Beery, half nodded to Granquist, sat down.

Kells said: "Drink?"

"Sure."

Kells looked at Granquist and she got up and went into the kitchen, came back with a bottle and a glass and handed them to Faber. He poured himself a drink.

118

Kells said: "Fenner isn't your boss any longer—how do you like that?"

Faber glanced at Borg, tipped the glass to his mouth, took it down when it was empty, said: "I like that fine."

"I want you to go to the Villa Dora out on Harper"—Kells looked up at Borg—"your car's still here, isn't it?"

Borg said: "Yeah."

"Take the car," Kells went on, "and hang on the front of that place until you see three big pigskin keesters go in and find out which apartment they go to. I don't know who'll have 'em, but there'll be three—and they'll probably come up in a closed Chrysler."

Faber said: "Uh huh." He picked up the bottle and poured himself another drink. He looked at Beery, then at the rest of them quickly. "Anybody else?"

Beery nodded; Granquist went out and got another glass.

Kells said: "Call here pronto—but I mean pronto. Spot a phone and call here the minute you connect. We'll be over right away and pick you up."

Faber nodded, drank. He put down his glass and stood up. "Villa Dora—that's below Sunset Boulevard, isn't it?"

Beery said: "Yes—between Sunset and Fountain."

Kells was looking out the window. "They'll probably come in between two this afternoon and nine tonight. You'd better get something to eat before you go out."

Faber said: "Okay." He put on his hat and said, "So long," and went out.

Beery smiled at Kells. "Are you going mysterious on me?"

"Those three cases are full of cocaine"—Kells was looking at Granquist—"according to my steer. A hundred and fifteen thousand dollars' worth—and there's a hundred and fifteen thousand dollars in cash waiting for them some place in the Villa Dora. It's Crotti's stuff and I have a hunch Max Hesse is on the buying end. I don't want the junk—I want the dough."

Beery stood up. He said: "Gerry—you're losing your mind. When you buck Crotti you're bucking a machine. They'll have a dozen guns trained on that deal—every angle figured—"

Granquist interrupted: "He's right. Gerry—you can't. . . ."

"What do *you* think about it?" Kells was staring morosely at Borg.

Borg put a black ten on a red Jack. "It'd be a nice lick," he said.

Kells put his leg down carefully, stood up. He held out his arm to Beery. "Give me a hand to the donnaker, Shep," he said.

Beery helped him across the room.

When Kells came back, Borg said: "The Doc called. He says he's sending over some crutches for you—an' for you to keep off that leg."

Beery helped Kells back to the big chair. He sat down and put his leg up on the other chair, muttered: "I don't want any——crutches."

Then he turned his head to smile at Granquist. "Isn't it about time you brought us all a drink, baby?"

Granquist got up and went into the kitchen.

Kells asked: "What time is it?"

Beery was standing beside Kells' chair. He glanced at his watch, held it down for Kells to see: eleven-five.

* * * * *

At eleven-twenty Woodward was announced. Granquist went into the bedroom and closed the door, and Borg let Woodward in.

Woodward's eyes were excited behind his wide-rimmed tortoise-shell glasses. He bowed nervously to Beery and Borg, sat down in the chair near Kells at Kells' invitation.

"How would you like to buy the originals of all the dirt on Bellmann?" Kells began.

Woodward smiled faintly. "We've discussed that before, Mister Kells," he said. "I'm afraid it's too late to do anything about it now—your *Coast Guardian* has published several of the pictures and the story. . . ."

Kells said: "You can doctor the negatives and claim they're forgeries—and I can give you additional information with which you can prove the whole thing was a conspiracy to blackmail Bellmann."

Woodward pursed his lips. He glanced at Beery, said: "Don't you think we might discuss this alone, Mister Kells?"

Kells shook his head shortly.

120

"In addition to all that," he went on, "the pictures and the information—I can give you"—he paused, leaned forward slightly—"absolute proof that Lee Fenner shot Bellmann."

Woodward's eyes widened a little. He leaned back in his chair and wet his lips, stared at Kells as if he weren't quite sure he had heard correctly.

"Lee Fenner killed Bellmann," Kells repeated slowly. He took a crumpled piece of paper out of the breast pocket of his dressing gown, straightened it out and tossed it on Woodward's lap.

Woodward picked it up and held it close to his face, put his hand up and adjusted his glasses. He put the paper back on the arm of Kells' chair in a little while, cleared his throat, said: "Who is Beery, who witnessed Fenner's signature with you?"

Kells inclined his head toward Beery, who was sitting at the table watching Borg's solitaire.

Woodward said: "How much do you want?"

"Plenty." Kells picked up the piece of paper, held it by a corner. He grinned at Beery. "It's lousy theater," he said. "The 'incriminating confession' "—he said it very melodramatically. "All we need is the 'Old Homestead,' some papier-mâché snow and a couple of bloodhounds."

"And you ought to have a black mustache." Beery looked up, smiled.

Woodward said: "As I told you—my, uh—people are pressed for cash."

"I don't give a damn how pressed they are. They can do business with me now—big business—and get their lousy administration out of the hole, or they can start packing to move out of City Hall. This is the last call. . . ."

Woodward started to speak and then the phone rang. Borg answered it, put his hand over the transmitter, nodded to Kells. Then he got up and brought the phone over.

Kells said: "Hello. . . . Wait a minute—I want you to meet a friend of mine."

He spoke to Woodward: "In case you're figuring this for a plant I want you to talk to this guy. You'd know Fenner's voice, wouldn't you?"

Woodward nodded. He took the phone from Kells, hesitantly said: "Hello."

Kells reached over and took the phone back. He smiled at Woodward, said: "Hello, Lee . . . That was Mister Woodward, a big buyer from downtown . . . Uh huh . . . Now don't get excited, Lee—we haven't made a deal yet . . . Why don't you come on over? . . . Yes—and bring plenty of cash—it starts at fifty grand . . . Okay, make it snappy."

He hung up, stared vacantly at Woodward's tie.

"Now I'm not going to argue with you," he said. "You heard what I told Fenner. You'd better get going—first here, first served."

Woodward stood up. "I'll see what I can do," he said. He put on his hat, nodded to Beery and Borg and started toward the door.

Kells said: "And don't get ideas. If you come back here with the law and try to hang a 'conspiracy to defeat justice' rap on me I'll swear that the whole god-damned thing is a lie—and so will my gentlemen friends." He jerked his head at Beery and Borg.

Woodward had turned to listen. He nodded, turned again and went out and closed the door.

Kells said: "This is going to be a lot of fun even if it doesn't work."

"You said something about being all washed up with the fun angle . . ." Beery got up and poured himself a drink. "You said something about being out for the dough."

"Watch it work." Kells leaned back in the chair and closed his eyes.

* * * * *

Fenner put thirty thousand-dollar notes on the arm of Kells' chair. Kells took the piece of crumpled paper out of his breast pocket and handed it to Fenner, and Fenner unfolded it and looked at it and then took a cigaret lighter out of his pocket and touched the flame to a corner of the paper.

Kells said: "Now get out of here while you're all together." He said it very quietly.

They were alone in the room.

Fenner said: "What could I do, Gerry? I *had* to go to Crotti when you told me he had this." He put the last charred corner of paper in an ash-tray. "It took me a couple of days to get to him—I was damned near crazy. . . ."

122

"Right." Kells moved his head slowly up and down and his expression was not pleasant. "You were plenty crazy when you offered Crotti my scalp."

Fenner stood up. He didn't say anything, just stood there looking out the window for a minute—then he turned and started toward the door.

"I'll give you a tip, Lee." Kells' voice was low; he stared with hard cold eyes at Fenner. "Take it on the lam—quick."

Fenner opened his mouth and then he closed it, swallowed.

He said: "Why—what do you mean?"

Kells didn't answer; he stared at Fenner coldly. Fenner stood there a little while and then he turned and went out. Borg and Granquist came out of the kitchen.

Kells said: "Thirty. I wonder if we'll do as well with Woodward. These guys don't seem to take me seriously when I talk about fifty thousand. Maybe it's the depression."

At a few minutes after one, Woodward telephoned.

The crutches that Janis had called about had been delivered and Kells was practicing walking with them. He put them down, sat down at the table and took the phone from Borg. He said, "Hello," and then listened with an occasional affirmative grunt. After a minute or so he said, "All right—make it fast," hung up.

He grinned at Granquist. "Twenty more. Up to now it's been a swell day's work. If we get it. . . ."

Borg said: "Do you mind letting me in on how the hell you're going to sell this thing to Woodward when you've already sold it to Fenner?"

Kells took two more pieces of creased crumpled paper from his pocket, tossed them on the table in front of Borg.

Borg looked at the two, smiled slowly. "How about making them up in gross lots?" he said.

Kells inclined his head toward Granquist. "The baby's work. She used to be in the business—she went over to the Lido early this morning and snagged the letterheads."

Granquist was sitting in the big chair by the window. Kells picked up the two pieces of paper and put them back in his pocket, got up and hobbled over to her, sat down on the arm of the chair.

123

"You're awfully quiet, baby," he said. "What's the matter?"

She looked up at him and her eyes were frightened.

"I want to go—I want us to go," she said huskily. "Something awful's going to happen. . . ."

Kells put his arm around her head, pulled it close against his chest.

"If we get the twenty from Woodward," he said very quietly—"and the big stuff from Crotti, it'll make almost two hundred grand—"

"We've got enough," she broke in. "Let's go, Gerry—please."

He sat without moving or speaking for a little while, staring out the window at the brightness of the sun. Then he got up and went back to the table and took up the phone and asked the operator to get him the Sante Fe ticket office.

When the connection had been made, he said: "I want to make reservations on the *Chief*, tomorrow evening—a drawing room—two. . . ."

Granquist had turned. She said: "Tonight, Gerry."

Kells smiled at her a little. He shook his head and said: "Yes . . . Kells, Miramar Apartments in Hollywood—send them out."

Then be hung up and reached across the table for the bottle and glasses, poured drinks. He raised his glass.

"Here's to Crime—and the *Chief* tomorrow night."

There was a knock at the outer door and Granquist went into the bedroom; Borg got up and let Woodward in.

Woodward was very nervous. He put two neat sheafs of thousand- and five-hundred-dollar notes on the table said: "There you are, sir."

Kells tossed one of the forged confessions across the table and slid one of the thousand-dollar notes out of the sheaf, examined it carefully.

Woodward said: "And the other things—the pictures and things? . . ."

"They're downtown. I'll call Beery to turn them over to you—at the Hayward."

Woodward nodded. He went over to the window and adjusted his glasses, peered closely at the paper. He turned to say something and then there was a sharp sound and glass tinkled on the floor. Woodward stood with his mouth open a little while, then his legs buckled under him slowly and he fell down and stretched one arm out and took hold the bottom of one of the drapes. He rolled his head once, back and forth, and his glasses came off and stuck out at an angle from the side of his head. His eyes were open, staring.

7

Kells said: "Well. . . ."

Borg was half standing. He moved his arm and very deliberately put the cards down on the table, then straightened, moved toward Woodward's body.

Kells said: "Don't go near the window."

Granquist came into the bedroom door and stood with one hand up to her face, staring at Woodward.

Borg said: "It must have been from that joint." He pointed through the window to the tall apartment house halfway down the block.

Kells said gently: "Bring me my clothes."

Granquist didn't move, stood staring at Woodward blankly.

Kells stood up. He said: "Bring me my clothes."

Borg went swiftly to the bedroom door, past Granquist into the bedroom, coming back almost immediately with a tangled mass of clothes under his arm. He held a short blunt revolver in one hand down straight at his side.

Granquist went to a chair against one wall and picked up her coat and put it on. She went to the table and stood with both hands on the table, leaning forward a little.

Kells sat down and took his clothes from Borg, one piece at a time, put them on.

The phone rang.

Kells picked it up, said: "Hello. . . . Shep—we're shoving off. Woodward's just been shot—through the window, from the roof of the place next door. . . . Uh hum. Maybe some of Crotti's boys tailed Fenner—your guess is as good as mine. . . . Call me in a half-hour at the Ambassador. If

I'm not there I'll be in jail—or on a slab. . . . Hell! No. Let 'em find him. . . . 'Bye."

He hung up, finished dressing rapidly, got up and limped to one side of the big window and pulled the cord that closed the drapes. Woodward's hand was clenched on the bottom of one of the drapes and it moved a little as the drape closed. The paper had fallen, lay a little way from his other hand.

Kells stood looking down at Woodward a minute, then went to the table and picked up the two thin stacks of money, put them in his pocket.

Borg had gone back into the bedroom. He came into the doorway and he had put on his shirt and coat, he went to a mirror near the outer door and carefully put on his hat.

Granquist picked up the crutches.

Kells shook his head, said: "My leg feels swell."

They went out into the corridor.

There was a man standing near the elevators but he paid no attention to them, entered one of the elevators while they were still halfway down the hall.

They waited a minute or so, got into the same elevator when it came back up. It was automatic—Kells pushed the sub-basement button.

He said: "Maybe. . . ."

Borg watched the sixth floor go by through the little wire-glass window. "The basement is as good a hunch as any," he said. "There's a garage with a driveway out onto Chero-kee. Maybe we can promote a car—or if we can get down to Highland, to the cab stand. . . ."

"Why didn't you call a cab?" Granquist was leaning back in a corner of the elevator.

Kells looked at her vacantly, as if he had not heard.

"Maybe this is a lot of apcray," he said—"maybe we're a cinch. But if that was Crotti"—he gestured with his head up toward the apartment—"he'll have a dozen beads on the place."

The elevator stopped and they went into a dark corridor, down to a door to the garage. There was a tall man with a very small mustache asleep in a big car near the archway that led out into Cherokee. He woke up when Borg stepped on the running board.

Borg asked: "How're chances of renting a car?"

The man rubbed his eyes, climbed out and stood between Kells and Borg. He said: "Sure. I got a Buick an' I got a Chrysler."

"Are either of them closed?" Kells leaned on Granquist's shoulder, winked at Borg meaninglessly.

The man said: "Yeah—the Buick."

He went toward a car five down the line from the one he had been sleeping in.

Kells said: "That'll do. How much deposit do you want?"

"You want a driver?"

"No."

Borg opened one rear door of the car and helped Granquist in. The man said: "No deposit if you live here. It's two an' a quarter an hour."

"Maybe we'll be out all night—you'd better take this." Kells gave the man two bills, got in through the front door carefully. He put his leg out straight under the dashboard.

Borg went around to the other side and squeezed in behind the wheel. He pressed the starter and the man reached in and pulled the choke and the engine roared; Borg scowled at the man and pushed the choke back in. They swung in a wide circle out through the archway into the sunlight.

Kells turned and spoke sharply to Granquist: "Lie down on the seat."

She muttered something unintelligible and lay down on her side across the back seat.

They turned swiftly down Cherokee and a spurt of flame came out of a parked, close curtained limousine to meet them, lead thudded, bit into the side of the car. Borg stepped on the throttle, they plunged forward, past.

Kells looked back at Granquist. She was lying with her eyes tightly closed and her face was very white. He put one arm back toward her and she rose suddenly to her knees, put her hands on his shoulder.

He smiled. "We're all right, baby," he said softly. "They build these cars in Detroit—that's machine-gun country."

Borg was crouched over the wheel. He spoke out of the side of his mouth: "Are they coming?"

Kells was looking back, shook his head. "They're turning around—they were parked the wrong way."

Granquist slid back to the seat.

They turned west on Yucca to Highland, jogged up Highland to Franklin, turned west on Franklin. They stopped between Sycamore and La Brea a little while and watched through the glass oval in the back of the car; the limousine had evidently been lost.

Borg got out and looked at the side of the car.

"It must have jammed," he said. "Four little holes, and a nick on one of the headlights. One of 'em missed the carburetor by about an inch—that was a break."

Kells said: "Let's go over and see how Faber is making out."

Borg climbed back into the car and they went on up Franklin to La Brea and down La Brea to Fountain. At the corner of Fountain and Harper they parked under a big pepper tree.

Kells turned around and spoke to Granquist: "You take the car—you can drive it, can't you?—and go down to the Ambassador and wait for us." He reached into his pocket, fished out a key. "Go up to my room and pack all the stuff that isn't already packed. Call up the Santa Fe and tell 'em to send the reservations there. If we get everything cleaned up tonight we'll drive down to San Bernardino and lay low tomorrow and get the *Chief* out of there tomorrow night."

Kells and Borg got out of the car and Granquist climbed over into the front seat. She said, "Be careful," without looking at Kells. She shifted gears and let the clutch in a little way and the car moved ahead.

Kells said: "Beery'll be calling in a little while. Tell him to come up to the hotel as soon as he can."

Granquist nodded without turning and the car moved ahead swiftly.

Kells and Borg crossed to the west side of Harper and walked slowly up toward Sunset Boulevard. Kells' limp was pronounced.

Borg asked: "How is it?" He bobbed his head at Kells' leg.

"All right."

They went slowly and without speaking up Harper, and a little way below the Villa Dora, Faber stuck his head out of Borg's car. They went over to it and Kells got into the ton-

128

neau and sat down; Borg stood outside, leaned on the front door.

Faber said: "Nothing yet."

Kells sat for several minutes staring absently at a long scratch on the back of the front seat. Then he said: "Let's go in and see what we can find." He leaned forward.

Faber lifted the flap of the right side pocket, slipped a black Luger out onto the seat beside him. He turned and looked at Kells and nodded at the gun. Kells reached over and took the gun and stuck it into the waistband of his trousers, pulled the point of his vest down over it.

"We're going in to try to find a hundred and fifteen grand in cash," he said. "I don't know who's got it—we'll have to try the mailboxes and see if we can get a lead."

Borg said: "We probably won't."

Kells opened the door and started to get out.

"Why don't you wait here and I'll see if I can find anything?" Borg took a light-colored cigar out of his outer breast pocket and bit off the end.

Kells looked at him a moment sleepily, nodded, sat down.

Borg went up the street and disappeared into the Villa Dora. He was back in a few minutes with a soiled envelope on which he had scrawled the names of the occupants.

Kells took it, looked at it, asked: "Are you sure this is all?"

"Yeah." Borg nodded. "It's a big joint, but I guess the apartments are big too—there are only twelve mailboxes."

Kells studied the names. Then he said: "MacAlmon—that's Bellmann's silksock ward heeler. I thought he lived in Beverly Hills." He stared at the envelope. "That'd be a tricky piece of business—if MacAlmon was go-between on the white stuff. I can figure his tie-up with Max Hesse—if Hesse is really the buyer—but how the hell would Crotti get to him?"

Faber looked interested at the mention of Crotti's name. He said: "Maybe this would be more fun for me if I knew what it was all about."

Borg said: "Crotti's delivering a load of C, and the hundred and fifteen we want to locate is what somebody up there"—he jerked his head toward the apartment house—"has got to pay for it with."

"Oh." Faber turned to Kells. "Count me out—I don't want any part of Crotti."

Kells smiled slowly. He said: "Okay."

Faber started to get out of the car and then he looked at Kells' hands; Kells had slipped the Luger out of his waistband, was holding it loosely on his lap.

Borg said: "Aw, for God's sake, cut it out." He looked from Kells to Faber.

Kells was smiling faintly at Faber. He said very seriously: "Your cut on this lick is ten grand. You've got *one* coming now—an' you can have it, but you'll have to stick around until this is over." He put his hand into his pocket and slid out a roll of bills, pulled one off and held it toward Faber.

Faber looked at it a little while, then he grinned sourly, said: "Well—if I've got to stay I might as well work." He took the bill, folded it carefully and put it into his watch pocket. "Deal me in—ten grand'll buy a lot of flowers."

"Me—I want to be cremated." Borg was staring soberly into space. "No flowers, but plenty of music." He glanced at Kells. "You know—Wagner."

Kells said: "Let's go and see if Mister MacAlmon is in."

He and Faber got out of the car and they all went up the street and into the Villa Dora.

*   *   *   *   *

Mister MacAlmon was in. He stood in the middle of his high-ceilinged living room with his hands in the air.

Kells said: "I'm sorry about this. I haven't anything against you or Hesse—if Hesse is in with you? But I've got plenty against Crotti and plenty against your whole bloody combination. I've been double-crossed to death. I'm goddamned tired of it—an' I need the dough."

MacAlmon was almost as tall as Kells. His thick brown hair was combed straight back from a high narrow forehead, and his eyes were dark, sharp.

He said: "This is plain robbery. How far do you think you're going to get with it?"

"Don't be silly." Kells looked at the stack of currency on the table. "I'll have the federal narcotic squad on their way out here in two minutes—and I'll see that you're here when they get here. Then all they'll have to do is wait for the stuff to come in. When you're pinched on a dope deal that's this big, see who you can get to listen to a squawk about money."

Borg was leaning against the outer door spinning the blunt revolver around his forefinger. Faber had waited outside.

Kells went to the telephone on a low round table, picked it up. "I've never called 'copper' on anybody in my life," he said. "But here it is. . . ." He spun the dial.

MacAlmon put his hand down. He said: "Wait a minute." He sat down in a big chair and leaned forward and put his elbows on his knees. He looked at Kells and his face was flushed and he tried very hard to smile. "Wait a minute."

Kells said into the telephone: "Information—what's the number of the Federal Building?" He waited a moment, said, "Thank you," pressed the receiver down with his thumb.

MacAlmon said: "How would you like to make twenty-five more?" He inclined his head toward the money on the table.

"This is enough." Kells shook his head. "All I want is a fair price for the time I've put in. This is it."

MacAlmon leaned back in the chair. "The stuff that's being delivered here this afternoon is worth exactly twice what's being paid for it, to me—my people," he said. "I don't care who gets the money—if you'll hold off until the transfer has been made and the stuff is in my possession I'll give you a twenty-five grand bonus."

Kells said: "No."

Someone knocked at the door.

Borg pressed his lips together and let his eyelids droop, shook his head sadly. He held the blunt, black revolver loosely in his hand and looked at Kells.

Kells framed the word, "Faber," with his lips. Borg kept on shaking his head. Kells took the Luger out of his belt and crossed the room and stood close to the wall; he nodded slightly to Borg.

Crotti and two other men came in. One of the men was carrying a big pigskin kitbag; one carried two. Crotti looked at MacAlmon and then he turned his head and looked at Borg. He hadn't seen Kells. The man with one bag put it down on the floor, straightened. Borg closed the door.

Kells said: "Hello."

The man who had been carrying one bag took one step sideways. At the same time he jerked an automatic out of a shoulder holster, sank to one knee and swung the automatic up toward Borg. Borg's gun roared twice.

Crotti had taken two or three steps forward. His head was turned toward Kells and his black wide-set eyes were big, his thick red mouth hung a little open.

The man with two bags still stood just inside the door. His small face was entirely expressionless; he bent his knees slowly and put down the bags. The other man looked up at Borg and his face was soft and childlike and surprised; then he toppled over on his side.

MacAlmon was standing up. Kells moved toward Crotti.

Borg was staring at Crotti: he moved suddenly forward, very swiftly for a fat man, and took the revolver barrel in his left hand and swung the gun back and brought it down hard on the back of Crotti's head. Crotti was still looking at Kells. His eyes went dull and he fell down very hard.

The man with two bags had turned and put his hand on the doorknob. Kells said, "Hey," and the man turned and stood with his back against the door.

Kells went to the door swiftly and reached past the man and turned the key in the lock and took it out and put it in his pocket. He went back to the table and put down the Luger, scooped the money up and stuffed it into his pockets. He glanced at MacAlmon, indicated the three kitbags with his eyes.

"Now you've got it. What are you going to do with it?"

MacAlmon was staring down at Crotti. Borg was watching the man at the door.

Kells said: "We're off!"

Borg went to the man at the door and patted his pockets, felt under his arms.

They went out through the kitchen, out through the service entrance into the hall. They heard someone pounding at the front door as they went out. They went down the hall, down the back stairs and out a side door to a small patio. At the street side of the patio Borg stood on a bench and looked over the wall. He shook his head and stepped down, said: "Faber's gone."

Kells said: "Maybe we can get through to the next street."

They went to the other end of the patio and through a gate to a kind of alleyway that led down to Fountain. They went down the alleyway and turned west on Fountain. They went into a drugstore on the corner and Kells drank a Coca-Cola while Borg called a cab.

While they were waiting for the cab Kells bought some aspirin, swallowed two tablets.

Borg said: "That's just a habit. That junk don't do you no good."

Kells nodded absently.

In a little while the cab came along.

*   *   *   *   *

Kells and Granquist and Beery and Borg sat in Kells' room at the Ambassador.

"Here's the laugh of the season . . ." Beery tilted his chair back against the wall. "The apartment at the Miramar was in Fenner's name. We had the maid service cut out—none of the help ever saw you there . . ."

Kells finished his drink, put the glass on a table.

Beery went on like a headline: "Fenner is being sought for questioning in connection with the Woodward murder."

Borg chuckled.

"And there's a warrant out for him for Bellmann's shooting on the strength of the confession they found on Woodward." Beery tilted his chair forward, reached for his glass. "The Woodward one is being blurbed as 'The Through the Window Murder.' "

Kells asked: "Who found the body?"

"Some glass from the window fell down into the driveway and somebody went up to find out who was carrying on."

Granquist said: "There must be something there they can trace to us." She didn't look very happy.

Kells glanced at her, grinned at Beery. "Miss Pollyanna G will now recite—"

She interrupted him: "Let's go, Gerry—please . . ." She stood up.

Kells said: "Buy us all a drink, baby."

He went on to Beery: "They'll probably trace us through Doc Janis—or telephone calls—or something."

Beery shook his head. "They'll be tickled to death to hang the whole thing on Fenner."

"Do you think they'll be so tickled they'll drop the case against me entirely?" Granquist turned from the table, came toward them with three tall glasses between her hands.

Kells said: "Shep and I will find out about that in about a half hour."

"And we'll find out what happened at MacAlmon's after you left." Beery stood up and took his drink from Granquist.

Someone knocked at the door.

Granquist froze, with a glass held out toward Borg; Beery opened the door and a porter came in.

He smiled, nodded to Kells. "You want your luggage to go down sir?"

Kells said: "Yes. The trunk's to go on the *Chief* tomorrow night. Put the other stuff where we can load it into a car."

The porter said: "Yes, sir." He tilted the trunk and dragged it out through the door. Beery went back and sat down.

Borg had taken his drink from Granquist. He said: "What I want to know is how the hell am I going to get my automobile."

Kells turned from the desk. "Will you please stop wailing about that wreck?" he said. He held out a singly folded sheaf of bills and Borg reached up and took it.

Kells went back to his chair, sat down and tossed another sheaf of bills in Beery's lap.

Beery looked down at it a moment, and then he picked it up and stuck it in his pocket, said: "Thanks, Gerry."

Granquist gave Kells one of the tall glasses. "Stirrup cup."

They all drank.

The porter came back into the room and loaded himself down with hand luggage, went out.

Kells said: "We're *all* in a swell spot. The baby here"—he nodded toward Granquist—"is still wanted for Bellmann's murder—maybe. Shep and I have got to go down and okay our signatures on Fenner's confession—and maybe they'll want to talk to me about Woodward, or what happened at

MacAlmon's, and if there's been any squawk from MacAlmon's they'll be looking for Fat." He grinned at Borg.

Beery took a long envelope out of his inside coat pocket, turned it over several times on his lap. "If this doesn't square any beef they can figure," he said, "I'm a watchmaker."

The porter came back into the room for the last of the hand luggage. They all finished their drinks and went out to the elevator, down to the cab stand.

They took two cabs. Kells and Beery got into the first one; Granquist and Borg got into another, and all the hand luggage was put in with them. Kells told the driver of the second cab to keep about a half-block behind them when they stopped downtown.

Then he went back to the other cab and got in with Beery and said: "Police Station."

*　*　*　*　*

Beery signed the affidavit and pushed it across the desk to Kells.

Captain Larson blew his nose. He said: "You understand you both will be witnesses for the state when we get Fenner?"

Kells nodded.

"An' this Granquist girl—she's a material witness too." The captain widened his watery blue eyes at Beery, leaned far back in his swivel chair.

Kells read the affidavit carefully, signed.

Larson said: "What do you know about the Woodward business?"

"Nothing." Kells put his elbow on the desk, his chin in his hand, stared at Larson expressionlessly. "I lost Fenner's confession shortly after it was signed—before I could use it. Woodward evidently got hold of it some way and was trying to peddle it back to Fenner."

"If Fenner was in his place at the Miramar when Woodward was shot, how come he left the confession there?" Larson was looking out the window, spoke as if to himself.

Kells shook his head slowly.

Larson said: "I suppose you know you're tied up with all this enough for me to hold you." He said it very quietly, kept looking out the window.

Kells smiled a little, was silent.

Beery leaned across the desk. "Fenner killed Bellmann," he said. "That's a swell break for the administration. It'd be even a better break if all the dirt on Bellmann that the *Coast Guardian* published was proven to be fake— wouldn't it?"

Larson turned from the window. He took a big handkerchief out of his pocket, blew his nose violently, nodded.

Beery took the long envelope out of his pocket and put it on the desk and shoved it slowly across to Larson.

"Here are the originals of the photographs and a couple of letters. You can burn 'em up and then challenge the *Coast Guardian* people to produce—or you can have 'em doctored so they'll look like phoneys."

Larson looked down at the envelope. He asked: "Who are the *Coast Guardian* people?"

Kells smiled, said: "Me—I'm them."

Larson slit the envelope, glanced at its contents. Then he put the envelope in the top drawer of his desk and stood up. Kells and Beery stood up, too. Larson reached across the desk and shook hands with them. They went out of the office, downstairs.

Kells said: "It looks like MacAlmon hasn't squawked— maybe he got away with the junk after all."

They passed the Reporters' Room and Beery said: "Wait a minute—maybe I can find out." He went in and telephoned and came out, shook his head. "Nothing yet."

Their cab was across the street. Kells looked up First Street to where the second cab had been parked on the other side of Hill Street. It had gone. He stood there a moment looking up First, then he said, "Come on," and crossed the street, asked the driver: "What happened to the other cab?"

The driver shook his head. "I don't know. It was there a minute ago an' then I looked up an' it was gone."

Kells got into the cab, stared through the open door at Beery. His face was hard and white. "We were going to an auto-rental joint over on Los Angeles Street and hire a car and driver to take us down to San Bernardino. But she didn't know the address—they couldn't have gone over there."

Beery said: "Maybe they were in a 'no parking' zone and had to go around the block."

A short gray-haired man came out on the steps of the Police Station and called across to Beery: "Telephone, Shep—says it's important."

Beery ran across the street and Kells got out of the cab and followed as fast as he could. That wasn't very fast; his leg was hurting pretty badly. When he went into the Reporters' Room, Beery was standing at a telephone, jiggling the hook up and down savagely, yelling at the operator to trace the call. Then he said: "All right—hurry it—this is the Police Station," hung up and looked at Kells.

The man who had called Beery to the phone glanced at them and then got up and went out into the hall.

They looked at one another silently for a moment and Beery sat down on one of the little desks. He said: "They've got her."

"Who?"

"I don't know—Crotti and MacAlmon I guess. You're supposed to do business with MacAlmon. . . ."

"What do you mean, business?" Kells was standing by one of the windows, his mouth curved in a hard and mirthless grin.

"They want their hundred and fifteen, and they want it quick. I don't know who I talked to—I couldn't place the voice. He said the price goes up twenty-five grand a day—and they'll send you one of her teeth every day, just to remind you. . . ."

Kells laughed. He looked out the window and laughed without moving his head, and the sound was cold and dry and rattling. He said: "To hell with it. Where did those saps get the idea she means that much to me? All she's given me is a lot of grief—I don't want any part of her."

Beery sat staring at Kells with a very faint smile on his lips.

"I'm in the clear—I've got mine. I'm going." Kells went unsteadily toward the door and then he turned and held out his hand. Beery stood up and took his hand and shook it gravely.

Kells said: "Why, goddamn it, Shep—she's double-crossed me a half dozen times. How do I know this isn't another one of those Scandinavian gags? She was Crotti's gal in the first place. . . ."

Beery nodded slowly. He said: "Sure."

Kells turned again toward the door. He took two or three steps and then he turned again and limped wearily over to one of the desks, sat down. He sat there a little while staring into space.

Then he said: "See if you can get MacAlmon, Shep."

Beery smiled, picked up the phone.

* * * * *

There were six men in MacAlmon's big living room at the Villa Dora. Crotti sat sidewise at a desk against one wall, leaned with one elbow on the big pink blotter that covered the desk. His thick red lower lip was thrust out, curved up at the corners in a fixed and meaningless smile.

There were two men sitting in straight-backed chairs on the other side of the room. One was Max Hesse. He was fat, ruddy-cheeked, blond; his suit looked as if it might have been cut out of a horse blanket. The other man was dark and slight. He fidgeted a great deal. He had been introduced simply as Carl.

Kells sat in one of the big armchairs near the central table and Beery sat on the edge of the table.

MacAlmon paced from the door to the table, back again.

Kells said: "Certainly not. You haven't got Granquist here—I haven't got the dough. Turn her over to me in the open and without any haggling and you can send anyone you want to a spot I'll give them, with an order from me. They can call you with an okay when they get the money. Then we'll walk."

Crotti moved his fixed smile from MacAlmon to Kells. He said: "You are very careful." The soft slurred impediment in his speech made it sound like a whisper.

Kells nodded without speaking, without looking at him.

Hesse laughed, a high dry cackle.

MacAlmon glanced at Crotti, then stopped his pacing, spoke to Kells: "She is here." He raised his eyes to the balcony that ran across half one side of the room. He called: "Shorty."

One of the three doors on the balcony opened and a squat over-dressed Filipino came out and leaned on the balustrade. He tipped his bright green velours hat to the back of his head, stared coldly, expressionlessly at MacAlmon.

MacAlmon said: "Bring her down."

The Filipino went back into the room and then came into the doorway with Granquist.

Her hair was loose, hung in straw-colored and angular disorder over her shoulders. Her eyes were wide, unseeing. A white silk handkerchief had been stuffed into her mouth, and her hands were knotted behind her back.

Kells said: "Take that god-damned gag out of her mouth." He spoke almost without moving his lips.

Beery stood up.

"I am very sorry." Crotti spoke sidewise to Kells. "She raised a lot of hell. . . ." He nodded to the Filipino.

The Filipino reached up delicately and flicked the handkerchief out of her mouth by one corner. She caught her breath sharply; her eyes rolled up whitely for a second then she closed them and swayed sideways with one hip against the balustrade.

Kells stood up slowly.

Crotti said: "Sit down."

Granquist opened her eyes and turned her head slowly and looked down at Kells. She opened her mouth a little and tried to speak. Then the Filipino took her arm and guided her down the stair, to a low chair between Kells and Crotti. She sank down into it, and the Filipino took a little knife out of his pocket and reached behind her and cut the twisted cord that held her hands. She leaned back and put her hands up to her face.

MacAlmon walked to the door and back.

Crotti asked: "How do you feel, sister?"

Granquist didn't move or show in any way that she had heard.

Kells sat down in the big chair, and Beery sat down again on the edge of the table.

Kells took a thin black card case out of his pocket and removed a card and spoke over his shoulder, to Beery: "Got a pencil?"

MacAlmon had come back from the door and was standing near Kells. He took a silver pencil out of his vest pocket, handed it to him. Hesse got up and went out into the kitchen and came back with a glass of water and put it down on the arm of Granquist's chair. He tapped her shoulder, smiled down at her. She took her hands away from her face a moment and stared blankly up at him, then she put her hands back over her eyes.

"How many men have you got outside?" Kells glanced at Crotti.

Crotti wasn't smiling any more. His wide-set eyes were very serious.

He said: "Two—one car." He took a dark green cigar out of his breast pocket, bit off the end, lighted it.

Kells was watching him, smiling faintly. Crotti looked up from lighting his cigar, nodded slowly, emphatically.

Hesse said: "I've got just my chauffeur—he is waiting. . . ."

Kells put the card down on the arm of his chair, scribbled something on it. He said: "You can send Carl, here"—he jerked his head toward the slight nervous man—"and whoever's outside after the dough. Berry will go along and tell 'em where to go." He was looking at Carl. "When you're paid off, Beery will call us here and you can okay it for your boss." He nodded at Crotti.

Crotti was smiling again. He said: "All right."

Carl got up and came over to pick up the card. Beery was at the telephone; he made a note of the number.

Kells went on: "Maybe the spick had better go along too."

The Filipino looked at him coldly. Crotti shook his head. Kells grinned, shrugged.

He said: "I'll see you later, Shep."

Beery nodded and put on his hat, went to the door with Carl. They went out.

Kells called to **Beery** as he was closing the door: "Tell that cab driver to sit on it—we'll be out in a little while."

MacAlmon went to a wall switch, snapped on several more lights. Then he went over and lay down on a wide divan under the big front windows. The drapes were tightly drawn.

Kells glanced at the tall clock in one corner. It was seven-fifty.

Hesse had taken MacAlmon's place at pacing up and down the floor.

Kells got up and limped to Granquist's chair, sat down on one arm of it and leaned close to her with his arm on her shoulder.

She whispered, "Gerry—I'm so sorry," without looking at him.

"Shut up, baby." He smiled down at her and pushed her hands gently down from her face.

"How's your leg?"

He said: "Swell." He patted his leg gingerly with one hand.

She moved her head over against his side. "It happened so damned quick," she said—"I mean quickly. They pulled up alongside of us and two of them got into the cab and stuck a rod into the driver and me and we came out here. Borg jumped out as soon as he saw them and ran down First Street—the car they came up in went after him. . . ."

Kells said: "He got away—he was waiting for us at the corner below the station. He's got the hundred and fifteen down at a little hotel on Melrose. That's where Shep's taking Crotti's boys. . . ."

Granquist sighed, whispered: "That's a lot of money."

Kells shook his head slowly. "That's the first really illegitimate pass we've made—maybe we didn't deserve it." He rubbed his forehead hard. "What happened to the cab with our stuff in it?"

"It's out in the driveway. They sapped the driver—he's upstairs sleeping it off."

They were silent a little while and then Kells said: "We forgot to send back the car we rented from the Miramar—remind me to do that as soon as we can."

"Uh huh." Granquist's voice was muffled.

Kells got up and went into the kitchen. He tried the back door, but it was locked and there was no key in it. When he came back Crotti had straightened around at the desk, was bent over it reading a paper.

Kells asked: "How's the fella my fat friend popped this afternoon?"

Crotti turned his head, nodded. "He's all right."

The phone rang and Kells answered it.

MacAlmon swung up to sit on the edge of the divan. Crotti turned slowly in his chair toward Kells. Hesse

141

stopped near the door. The Filipino was tilted back in a chair near the stairway that led up to the balcony and the room upstairs; his hat was pulled down over his eyes and he did not move.

Kells said, "Yes, Shep," into the telephone. He listened a little while and his face was cold and hard, his eyes were heavy. Then he said, "All right," and hung up the receiver.

He spoke, more to Granquist than to any of the rest of them: "Borg's gone."

Granquist leaned forward slowly.

Hesse said: "Who's Borg?"

"The guy who's got your money." Kells smiled slowly at Hesse. Then he glanced at the Filipino and there was a black automatic in the Filipino's hand. He was still tilted back against the wall and his hat almost covered his eyes.

Crotti stood up. He moved a little toward Kells and then stood very straight and stared at Kells and the muscles of his deeply lined white face twitched a little. He shook his head almost imperceptibly at the Filipino.

He said slowly: "No—I will do it myself, Shorty."

He put his hand to his side under the arm, under his coat, and took out a curiously shaped German revolver. He held it down straight at his side for a moment and then raised it toward Kells. He raised it as if he would like to be raising it very slowly and deliberately, but couldn't; he raised it very swiftly.

Kells' shoulders were hunched together a little. His chin was in and he looked at Crotti's feet and his eyes were almost closed.

Granquist stood up and her face was dead white, her hands were clawed in front of her body. She made no sound.

Then there was a sharp crashing roar. It beat twice, filled the room with dull sound.

Kells still stood with his shoulders a little together, his eyes almost closed.

Crotti swayed once to the left. His expression was querulous, worried; the revolver fell from his hand, clattered on the floor. One of his legs gave way slowly and he slipped down on one knee, fell slowly heavily forward on his face.

Kells turned his head swiftly, looked up. Borg was grinning down at him from the balcony; the short blunt blue revolver was lisping smoke in his hand. The Filipino was bent over, holding his wrist between his hand and knees. He whirled slowly on one foot—his hat had fallen off and his broad flat face was twisted with pain.

Borg said: "By God! Just like they do in the movies."

Hesse was at the door.

Borg swung the revolver around toward him, said: "Wait a minute."

MacAlmon hadn't moved. He was still sitting on the edge of the divan, staring at Crotti.

Kells said: "Let's go."

* * * * *

They stopped at a drugstore near Sixth and Normandie. Borg pulled up ahead of them in the other cab, and he and the driver transferred Kells' luggage to the one cab.

Kells said to the driver: "You can call up and report where this cab is if you want to." He gestured toward the second cab. "The driver is out at the joint we just left—Apartment L."

Borg said: "Maybe. They're probably all out of there by now."

"They wouldn't take the driver."

"They might—he could testify against 'em."

Kells and the driver went into the drugstore to telephone. Kells called Beery at home, said: "Swell, Shep. . . . Did you have any trouble getting away? . . . That's fine. . . . Borg got to worrying about giving all that dough back so he ducked over to MacAlmon's place and climbed in a window. . . . Uh huh. The crazy bastard damn near got me the works, but if he hadn't been there I wouldn't be here—so what? . . . I don't know whether to give him a punch in the nose or a bonus . . . I have an idea Crotti would've tried to smack me down whether Borg had been there to put the cash on the line or not. I don't think he liked me very well . . . So long, Shep, and good luck—I'll send you a postcard."

He hung up and went out and got into the cab with Granquist and Borg.

The driver turned around, asked: "Where to?"

"How'd you like to make a long haul?" Kells glanced at Granquist, smiled at the driver.

The driver said: "Sure. The longer the better."
Kells said: "San Bernardino."
He leaned back and closed his eyes.

8

The room was about thirty by fifteen. There were six booths along each long side. At one end there was a door leading to a kind of kitchen and at the other end there was a door that led to steps down to the alley. There was a small radio on a table beside the door that led to the kitchen and there was a clock on the wall above the table. It was five minutes past nine.

Kells and Granquist and Borg sat in the third booth on the right, coming in. There was no one in any of the other booths.

The cab driver went back to the door to the kitchen and called: "Jake." Then he bent over the radio, snapped it on.

A man came out of the kitchen, said "Hi" to the driver, came up to the booth. He was a tall man, about fifty-five, with a long crooked nose, a three- or four-day growth of gray beard. He wiped his hands on his dirty gray-white apron.

Kells asked: "Do you know how to make a whiskey sour?"

The man grinned with one side of his mouth, nodded.

"Oke—and put some whiskey in it."

Granquist was rubbing powder onto her nose, holding her head back and looking into a small mirror which she held in one hand, a little higher than her head.

She said: "Me too—an' ham and eggs."

Borg had slid low in the seat. His chin was on his chest and his eyes were closed. He asked, "Got any buttermilk?" without moving or opening his eyes.

The man shook his head.

Kells said: "Give him a whiskey sour, too—and give all of us ham and eggs. *Fresh* eggs."

He raised his head, called to the driver: "Is that all right for you?"

144

A dance orchestra blared suddenly out of the radio. The driver turned his head, smiled, nodded.

Jake went back into the kitchen.

Granquist called to the driver: "See if you can get Louie Armstrong."

Jake stuck his head through the door, said: "He don't come on till eleven." His head disappeared.

Kells grinned at Granquist.

She said: "Let's dance."

"Don't be silly." He glanced down at his leg.

"Oh, I'm sorry, darling." Her face was suddenly serious, concerned. "How is it?"

He shook his head without looking at her, was silent; after a minute or so he watched Jake come in with four tall glasses on a scarred tin tray.

Jake put the tray on the table, spoke over his shoulder to the driver: "Turn 'er down to ten—that's K G P L the police reports to the radio cars." He went back toward the kitchen. "Last night they held up the gas station down on the corner an' we knew it here, right away. I went downstairs an' saw the bandit car go by—sixty miles an hour." He jerked his head violently up and to the left, an unspoken "By Crackey!"

The driver turned the dial, then came to the booth and took one of the tall glasses. He sat down on the table directly across the narrow room, said, "Here's mud in your eye," drank.

It was quiet a little while, except for the hiss of frying eggs in the kitchen.

Then the radio hummed slowly, buzzed to words: "K G P L—Los Angeles Police Department. . . . Calling car number one thirty-two—car number one three two. . . . At Berkeley and Gaines streets—an ambulance follow-up. . . . That is all. . . . . Gordon."

Granquist held her glass in both hands, her elbows on the table. She tipped the glass, drank, said: "Not bad. Not *good*, but not bad."

Kells raised his head, called: "Bring out the bottle, Jake."

Borg opened his eyes, stared gloomily at his drink.

The radio sputtered to sound: "K G P L . . . Attention all cars—attention all cars. . . . Repeat as of eight-fifteen on

Crotti killing. . . . Persons wanted are: Number One—
Gerard A Kells. Description: six foot one—a hundred an'
sixty pounds—about thirty-five—red hair—sallow complex-
ion—wearing a dark blue suit, black soft hat—walks with a
limp, recent leg wound. . . ."

Jake came out of the kitchen carrying a bottle of whiskey
by the neck. He put it on the table and Kells took out the
cork and tipped the bottle, sweetened Granquist's, Borg's
and his own drink. He waved the bottle at the driver. The
driver slid off the table and came over and held out his glass
and Kells poured whiskey into it. The driver went back and
sat down on the table and Jake went back into the kitchen.

He said, "Ham an' eggs coming up," over his shoulder as
he went through the door.

The radio droned on: "Number Two—a woman, thought
to be Miss Granquist—first name unknown—also wanted in
connection with Bellmann murder. Description: five eight—
a hundred an' twenty pounds—twenty-seven—blonde—
high color. . . . Number Three—Borg—Otto J. Description:
five six—a hundred an' ninety pounds—forty—sandy com-
plexion. . . . Particular attention cars on roads out of Los
Angeles: these people are probably trying to get out of
town. . . . Don't take any chances—they're dangerous. . . . That is all. . . . Gordon."

The driver put his glass down, slid off the table. He said,
"I forgot to turn off my lights," started toward the door.

Borg said: "Sit down." He had not raised his head or
straightened up in his seat. The heavy snub-nosed revolver
glittered in his left hand.

Kells stood up slowly, squeezed out of the booth and
limped back to the kitchen door. He stood in the doorway
and said: "You can put that phone down and bring out our
ham and eggs now."

He continued to stand in the doorway until Jake came out
past him with four orders of ham and eggs on a big tray.
Jake's nose and forehead were shiny with sweat. He put
the tray on the table and stood wiping his hands on his
apron.

The driver turned and went back and sat down on the
table. He was very pale and there was a weak smile on his
face. He picked up his drink.

Borg gestured with his head and Jake went over and sat down in the booth with the driver.

Kells went into the kitchen.

Granquist's eyes were hard, opaque. She took one of the plates of ham and eggs off the tray, sat staring down at it.

Kells' voice came from the kitchen: "Madison two four five six. . . . Hello—*Chronicle?* . . . City desk, please. . . . Hello—is Shep Beery there? . . ."

Then he lowered his voice and they could not hear.

He called another indistinguishable number, talked a long time in a low voice.

Granquist ate mechanically. Borg finished his drink, got up and handed the driver's plate across to him. The driver sat down beside Jake, sliced the fried ham into thin strips.

After a while Kells came in and sat down. He pushed his plate away, poured whiskey into the glasses on the table.

He said quietly: "They've picked up Shep."

No one said anything. Granquist tipped her glass and Borg stared expressionlessly at Kells.

"And they've been tipped to our reservations on the *Chief* tomorrow night—they're watching all trains, all roads—they'll ride that train to Albuquerque." Kells drank. He looked at Granquist, then slowly turned his head and looked at Borg. "And they've tied us up with Abner here—or his bus." He moved his head slightly toward the cab driver.

Borg said: "Beery's talked."

"No." Kells shook his head slowly. "No. I don't think so."

Granquist put down her glass. "Don't be a sap, Gerry," she said—"he has."

Kells leaned across the table and slapped her very sharply across the mouth.

She stared at him out of wide, startled eyes and put her hands up to her face, slowly. Kells looked at her mouth, and his face was very white, his eyes were almost closed.

Borg was sitting up very straight.

Kells' hand was lying palm up on the table. Granquist put out one hand slowly and touched his and then she said, "I'm sorry," very softly.

Kells shook his head sharply, closed his eyes for a moment, then opened them and looked down at the table.

He said: "I'm sorry too, baby." He patted the back of her hand.

He stood up and leaned against the back of the booth, stared a long minute at Jake and the driver.

The driver looked up from his plate, said: "Ain't we goin' on to San Berdoo?"

Kells didn't show that he had heard. His eyes were blank, empty. He spoke sidewise to Borg: "I'm going back into town and find out what it's all about."

Granquist stood up swiftly. Her eyes were very bright and her face was set and determined. She said: "So am I."

Kells bent his head a little to one side. "You're going to stay here—and Fat is going to stay here. If I don't make out, I'll get a steer to you over the radio—or some way." He moved his eyes to Borg. "You snag a car and take her to Las Vegas or some station on the UP where you can get a train."

Borg nodded.

"I'm going to find out what happened to the immunity we were promised by Beery's pal, the captain," Kells went on. "He's supposed to have the chief of police in his pocket—and the D A is his brother-in-law." He poured a drink. "Now he puts the screws on us for knocking over Crotti. Public Enemy Number One." He drank, smiled without mirth. "God! That's a laugh."

Kells glanced at Granquist, moved his head and shoulders slightly, turned and went out into the kitchen. She followed him. He was half sitting on a big table and she went to him and put one arm around his shoulders, one hand on his chest. She moved her head close to his.

He spoke very quietly, almost whispered: "I've got to go by myself, baby. It's taking enough of a chance being spotted that way—it'd be a cinch if we were together."

"Can't we wait here till it cools off, or take a chance on getting away now?" Her eyes were hot and dry; her voice trembled a little.

Kells said: "No. That'd mean getting clear out of the country—and it'd mean being on the run wherever we were. I had that once before and I don't want any more of it."

He took a small package wrapped in brown paper out of his inside breast pocket and handed it to her. "There's somewhere near a hundred and ninety grand here," he said.

"Don't let Borg know you've got it. I think he's okay but that's a lot of money."

She took the package and put it in one of the big pockets of her long tweed topcoat.

Kells asked: "Have you got a gun?"

She nodded, patted her handbag. "I picked up the spick's—the guy who was with Crotti."

Kells kissed her. He said: "I'll get word to you some way, or be back by tomorrow noon. Watch yourself."

He limped to the door, through it into the other room.

Granquist followed him to the door, stood leaning against the frame; her face was dead white and she held her deep red lower lip between her teeth.

Kells spoke over his shoulder to the driver: "Come on."

The driver jumped up and followed him to the outer door.

Kells turned at the door, said, "Be seeing you," to Borg. He did not look at Granquist. He went out and the driver went out after him and closed the door.

*   *   *   *   *

On Kenmore near Beverly Boulevard Kells leaned forward and tapped on the glass. The cab swung to the curb and the driver slid the glass. Kells asked: "Are you married?"

The driver looked blank for a moment, then said: "Uh huh—only we don't get along very well."

Kells smiled faintly in the darkness. "Maybe you'd get along better if you took her for a little vacation down to Caliente—or Catalina." He held out four crumpled bills and the driver reached back and took them. He held them in the dim light of the taxi meter and whistled, and then he stuck the bills hurriedly in his pocket and said: "Yes, sir."

Kells said: "I want you to remember that you took us up to Lankershim and that we transferred to another car there and headed for Frisco. Is your memory that good?"

"Yes, sir." The driver nodded emphatically.

"If it isn't," Kells went on—"I give you two days. My friends here would be awfully mad if anything happened to me on account of your memory slipping up." He lowered his voice, spoke each word very distinctly: "Do you understand what I mean?"

The driver said: "Yes, sir—I understand."

Kells got out and stood at the curb until the cab had turned down Beverly, disappeared. Then he went to the drugstore on the corner and called the taxi stand at the Ambassador, asked if Number Fifty-eight was in. He was on a short trip, was expected back soon. Kells left word for Fifty-eight to pick him up on Beverly near Normandie, went out of the drugstore, west.

His leg didn't hurt so badly now. He wasn't quite sure whether it was a great deal hotter or only momentarily numb. Anyway, it felt a lot better—he could walk fairly comfortably.

The cab detached itself from northbound traffic at the corner of Normandie, pulled into the curb. Fifty-eight stuck his head out and grinned at Kells.

Kells climbed into the cab, asked: "H' are ya?"

Fifty-eight said: "Swell—an' yourself? Where to?"

"Let's go out to the apartment house on the corner of Yucca and Cahuenga first." Kells leaned back.

They went over Normandie to Franklin, west on Franklin to Argyle, down the curve of Argyle and west two more blocks to Cahuenga. Kells got out, said, "I won't be long," and went into the apartment house on the corner. He asked at the desk for the number of Mister Beery's apartment, went into the elevator and pressed the third-floor button.

Florence Beery was tall—almost as tall as Kells—slim. Her hair was very dark and her eyes were big, heavily shadowed. She stood in the doorway and looked at Kells, and her face was a hard, brittle mask.

She said slowly: "Well—what do you want?" Her voice was icy, bitter.

Kells put up one arm and leaned against the doorframe. He asked: "May I come in?"

She looked at him steadily for a moment, then she turned and went through the short hallway into the living room. He closed the door and followed her into the living room, sat down. She stood in the center of the room, staring at the wall, waiting.

Kells took off his hat and put it on the divan beside him. He said: "I'm sorry about Shep—"

"Sorry!" She turned her head toward him slowly. Her eyes were long upward-slanted slits. "Sorry! This is a hell

150

of a time to be sorry!" She swayed a little forward.

Kells said: "Wait, Florence, Shep wouldn't be in the can if he hadn't thrown in with me. He wouldn't be ten or twelve grand ahead, either. The dough hasn't been so hard to take, has it?"

She stood staring at him with blank unseeing eyes, swaying a little. Then she sobbed and the sound was a dry, burnt rattle in her throat, took two steps toward him, blindly. She spoke and it was as if she were trying to scream—but her throat was too tight, her words were low, harsh, like coarse cloth tearing:

"God damn you! Don't you know Shep is dead—dead!"

The word seemed to release some spring inside her—sight came to her eyes, swift motion to her body—she sprang at Kells, her clawed hands outstretched.

He half rose to meet her, caught one of her wrists, swung her down beside him. The nails of her free hand caught the flesh of his cheek, ripped downward. He threw his right arm around her shoulders, imprisoned her wrists in his two hands, then he took her wrists tightly in his right hand, pressed her head down on her breast with his left. She was panting sharply, raggedly. Then she relaxed suddenly, went limp against his arm—her shoulders went back and forth rhythmically, limply—she was sobbing and there was no sound except sharp intake of breath.

Kells released her gradually, gently, stood up. He walked once to the other side of the room, back. His eyes were wide open and his mouth hung a little open, black against the green pallor of his face. He sank down beside her, put his arm again around her shoulders, spoke very quietly: "Florence. For the love of Mary!—when?—how?"

After a little while she whispered without raising her head: "When they were taking him to the Station—from a car—they don't know who it was. . . ."

Kells was staring over her shoulder at a flashing electric sign through the window. His eyes were glazed, cold—his mouth twitched a little. He sat like that a little while and then he took his arm from around her shoulders, picked up his hat and put it on, stood up. He stood looking down at her for perhaps a minute, motionlessly. Then he turned and went out of the room.

It was ten-fifty when the cab swung in to the curb in front of a bungalow on South Gramercy.

Fifty-eight turned around, said: "You'd better be wiping the blood off your face before you go in, Mister Kells."

Kells mechanically put the fingers of his left hand up to his cheek, took them away wet, sticky. He took out a handkerchief and pressed it against his cheek, got out of the cab and went toward the dark house.

After he had rung the bell four or five times, a light was switched on upstairs, he heard someone coming down. The lower part of the house remained dark, but a light above him—in the ceiling of the porch—snapped on. He stood with his chin on his chest, his hat pulled down over his eyes, watching the bottom of the door.

It opened and Captain Larson's voice said: "Come in," out of the darkness. Kells went in.

The light on the porch snapped off, the light in the room snapped on. The door was closed.

It was a rather large living room which, with the smaller dining room, ran across all the front of the house. The furniture was mostly Mission, mostly built-in. The wall paper was bright, bad.

Larson stood with his back to the door in a nightshirt, big, fleece-lined slippers. He held a Colt .38 revolver steadily in his right hand. He said: "Take a chair."

Kells sat down in the most comfortable looking chair, leaned back. Larson pulled another chair around and sat down on its edge, facing Kells. He leaned forward, put his elbows on his knees—he held the revolver in his right hand hanging down between his legs, said: "What's on your mind?"

Kells tipped his hat back a little and stared at Larson sleepily.

"You gave me a free bill this afternoon," he said, "in exchange for some stuff that would have split your administration—your whole political outfit—wide open." He paused, changed his position slightly. "Now you clamp down on me because somebody gets the dumb idea I had something to do with the Crotti chill. What's the answer?"

"Crotti's the answer." Larson spat far and accurately into

152

the fireplace, wiped his mouth on his sleeve. He leaned back and crossed his legs and held the revolver loosely in his lap. "There's a lot of water been under the bridge since I seen you this afternoon," he went on. "In the first place I didn't give you no free bill, as you call it—I told you that you and your gal would probably be wanted for questioning in connection with a lot of things. An' I hinted that if you wasn't around when question time came we wouldn't look too far for you." He took a crumpled handkerchief from the pocket of his nightshirt, blew his nose gustily. "Crotti's something else again."

Kells smiled slowly. "Crotti was your Number One Gangster," he said. "If I *had* something to do with his killing I ought to be getting a medal for it—not a rap."

A woman's cracked querulous voice came down the stairs: "What is it, Gus?"

Larson spat again into the fireplace, looked at the stairs. "Nothin'. Go back to bed."

He turned back toward Kells and his big loose mouth split to a wide grin. "You're way behind the times," he said. "Crotti hooked up with my people this morning. They were tickled to death to get an organization like his behind them and they were plumb disappointed when you bumped him off. That's *one* of the reasons there's a tag out for you. . . ."

Kells held his handkerchief to his bleeding cheek. He said: "What are the other reasons?"

"Jack Rose moved into Crotti's place."

Kells laughed soundlessly. "You're kidding."

"No." Larson spun the revolver once around his big forefinger. "Rose made a deal with Crotti a couple of days ago. When Crotti was shot this evening, Rose didn't lose any time putting the pressure on my people and they didn't lose any time putting it on me. You're it."

"But Rose is wanted for the O'Donnell—"

"Not any more." Larson chuckled. "I told you you wasn't keeping in touch with things. For one thing, Lee Fenner shot himself about eight o'clock tonight. He was the only one there was to testify against Rose on the O'Donnell angle—so that's out. And Rose says *you* killed O'Donnell, says he'll swear to it—an' he's got another witness."

Kells said wearily: "Is that all—I'm only wanted on two counts of murder?"

"That's all for tonight. Matheson called me up a couple hours ago an' said the Perry woman had phoned in, drunk, an' said she wanted to repudiate her confession that Perry killed Doc Haardt." Larson grinned broadly, stood up. "Maybe we can tie you up to that in the morning."

He took two sidewise steps to a small stand and picked up the telephone receiver with one hand, squatted down until his mouth was near the transmitter. He held the revolver in his right hand, watched Kells closely while he spoke into the phone:

"Gimme Michigan six one one one, sister. Uh huh . . . Hello, Mike—this is Gus . . . Kells is out here—out at my house . . . Come on out an' get him . . . Uh huh."

He hung up the receiver, stood up and went back to the chair and sat down.

"You been mixed up in damn near every killing we had the past week," he said. "It looks to me like you been our Number One Gunman—not Crotti."

Kells leaned forward slowly.

Larson said: "Sit still."

Kells asked: "What do you think my chances are of getting to the Station on my feet?"

"Wha' d'you mean?" Larson was blowing his nose.

"I mean they got Beery on the way in after he'd been pinched tonight. I mean your desk sergeant has tipped Rose that I'm out here by now—he'll be here by the time your coppers are—will be waiting outside. They'll take me in to a slab."

Larson said: "Aw, don't talk that way." He squinted his eyes as if he were trying to remember something, then said proudly: "You got a prosecution complex, that's what you got—a prosecution complex."

Kells stood up.

Larson jerked his head emphatically at the chair, snapped: "Sit down."

Kells said slowly: "I work pretty fast, Gus. I'll bet you can shoot me through the heart an' I'll have my gun out an' have a couple slugs in your belly before I hit the floor." He smiled a little. "Let's try it."

Larson said, "Sit down," loudly.

"I'll bet you can't even hit my heart—I'll bet you're a lousy shot." Kells took a short step forward, balanced himself evenly on both feet.

Larson was white. His big mouth hung a little open.

Kells said: "Let's go." His hand went swiftly to his side.

Larson's shoulders moved convulsively, his right hand went forward, up, with the revolver. At the same time he threw his head forward and down, fell forward out of the chair. The revolver clattered on the floor.

Kells was standing on the balls of his feet, an automatic held crosswise against his chest. He stared down at Larson and his eyes were wide, surprised.

He said, "Well, I'll be god-damned," under his breath.

Larson was on his hands and knees; his big shoulders and thick neck were pulled in tightly, rigidly.

Kells stooped and picked up the revolver, stuck it into his overcoat pocket. Then he laughed quietly, said: "Copper yellow. That's the first time my reputation ever did me any good."

He went to the door swiftly, turned once to glance hurriedly at Larson. Larson had risen to his knees. He did not look at Kells; he looked at the wall—he was breathing heavily.

Kells opened the door and went out and closed it behind him.

* * * * *

Fifty-eight said: "There it is."

They were parked in the deep shadow between two street lights in the next block to the one Larson's house was in. A big touring car had come up quietly, without lights, stopped across the street from Larson's.

Kells didn't say anything. He sat huddled in a corner of the cab and although the night was fairly warm he shivered a little.

After a few minutes another car swung around the corner, pulled up in front of Larson's. Kells leaned forward and watched through the glass. Three men got out and went into the house. In a little while they came out; one of them went across the street and stood beside the car that had come up first, the others got into the other car and drove away.

Then the man got into the second car, its lights were switched on and it too drove away.

Kells said: "Give 'em enough room."

Fifty-eight waited until the other car was more than half-way down the long block, let the clutch in slowly. Kells felt in his pockets until he found the tin box of aspirin tablets, took two. The other car turned left on Third Street. Fifty-eight stepped on it, swung into Third; there were two tail-lights about a block and a half ahead. He followed the faster one north on Rossmore, got close enough to see that he'd guessed right, fell back.

They turned west again on Beverly, to La Brea.

Kells was sitting sideways on the seat looking through the rear window. He leaned forward suddenly, spoke rapidly to Fifty-eight: "Keep that car in sight—an' you'll have to do it by yourself. I've got something else to watch. We're being tailed."

They turned off La Brea, west on Santa Monica Boulevard.

Then Kells was sure they were being followed. The car was a big blue or black coupé—shiny, powerful.

On Santa Monica, a little way beyond Gardner, Fifty-eight said over his shoulder: "They're stopping."

"Go on past 'em—slow."

Kells squeezed back into the corner, saw four men get out of the touring car and start across the street. He thought one of them was Detective Lieutenant Reilly; wasn't sure. He didn't recognize any of the others.

Fifty-eight asked: "What'll I do?"

"Go on—slow." Kells took the automatic from its shoulder holster, balanced it across his hand. He watched the big coupé come up slowly.

It overtook them in the second block, stayed alongside.

Kells said: "Turn off right, at the next side street." He was deep in the dark corner of the cab, watching the coupé narrowly. Then the driver of the coupé put up his hand and Kells saw that it was Borg. They turned together into the side street, drove up about a hundred yards to comparative darkness. Borg parked a little way ahead of the cab.

Kells got out and went up to the coupé. He said. "That's the way people have accidents," unpleasantly.

Borg was silent.

Granquist was sitting very low in the seat beside Borg. She straightened, said: "Your other driver spilled his guts an' the tip went out on the joint we were at—"

Borg interrupted her: "That's a swell invention, the radio. I don't know what we would've done without it."

"Then while we were getting out," Granquist went on, "the call went out to the car in Larson's neighborhood to go and pick you up—we got the address from that. Fat couldn't find a car so we hired this one at a garage—"

"An' damn' near busted our necks getting to Larson's," Borg finished.

Kells asked: "Where did you pick me up?"

"We were turning off Third onto Gramercy when you turned into Third." Borg lighted his stump of cigar. He bent his head toward Granquist. "Miss Eagle-eye here thought she spotted you in the cab—an' I thought she was nuts. She wasn't."

"Did you know I was following another car?"

Granquist said: "Sure."

"That was one of Rose's cars." Kells put one foot on the running board, leaned on the door. "It was planted across from Larson's to smack me down when the cops brought me out." He hesitated a moment. "That's what happened to Shep when they were taking him in."

Borg swallowed, started to speak: "They . . ."

Granquist said: "Gerry—for God's sake get in and let's get out of here." Her voice was low; she spoke very rapidly. "Please, Gerry, let's go now—we can make the Border by three o'clock."

"Sure. In a little while." Kells was looking at the black and yellow sky.

It began to rain a little.

Borg said: "So what?"

"That car stopped at Ansel's." Kells jerked his head back toward Santa Monica Boulevard. "Ansel runs a cheap crap game that's backed by Rose—I've been there. It's a pretty safe bet that Rose is there, and his carload of rods went back there to report to him."

Borg said: "Uh huh. So, what?"

Kells stared at Borg vacantly. "So I'm going up an' tell Rose about Beery—about Beery's wife."

Granquist opened the door suddenly, got out on the sidewalk on the other side of the car. She held her arms stiff at her sides and her hands were clenched; she was trembling violently. She walked up the sidewalk about thirty feet—walked as if she were making a tremendous effort to walk slowly. Then she turned and leaned against a telephone pole and looked back at the car.

Kells watched her; he could not see her face in the darkness, only the dim outline of her body. He turned slowly to Borg.

"You can wait here," he said. "Or maybe you'd better wait down at the first corner this side of Ansel's. And stay with the car—both of you."

Borg said: "All right."

Kells walked up to Granquist. He stood looking down at her a little while, asked: "What's the matter, baby?"

Her voice, when she finally answered, was elaborately sarcastic. "What's the matter? What's the matter?" Then her tone changed abruptly—she put one trembling hand on his arm. "Gerry—don't do this," she said. "Let it go—please this time. . . ."

He was smiling a little. He shook his head slightly.

She took her hand from his arm and her voice was suddenly acid, metallic. "You—and your pride! Your long chances—your little tin-horn revenge!" She laughed shrilly, hysterically. "You've seen too many gangster pictures—that's what's wrong with you. . . ."

Kells was staring at her expressionlessly. He turned abruptly, strode back toward the car.

She was behind him, sobbing, trying to hold his arm.

"Gerry!" Her words, were blurred, broken. "Gerry—can't you think of me a little—can't you let this one thing go—for me? For us?"

He shook her hand off, spoke briefly to Borg: "An' stay with the car this time—I'll be wanting it in a hurry, when I want it."

Borg said: "Oke. First corner this side of the joint."

Kells went back to the cab, got in, said: "Take me down to Gardner, about a half-block the other side of the Boulevard."

Fifty-eight grunted affirmatively and swung the cab around in the narrow street.

158

Kells glanced back through the rear window. Granquist was standing motionlessly in the middle of the street, silhouetted against the glow of a street light on the far corner.

It began raining harder, pounded on the roof of the cab. Fifty-eight started the windshield wiper and it swished rhythmically in a wide arc across the glass.

They stopped in the shelter of a big palm on Gardner and Kells got out.

Fifty-eight asked: "Can I help, Mister Kells?"

Kells shook his head. "I'll make out." He peeled two bills off the roll in his pocket, handed them to the little Irishman. He turned swiftly and went into the darkness between two houses, heard Fifty-eight's "Thank you, sir," behind him.

The driveway ended in a small garage; there was a gate at one side leading to a kind of narrow alley. Kells crossed the alley and walked north along a five-foot board fence for about a hundred feet. Then he climbed over the fence and went across a vacant, weed-grown lot toward the rear end of the building that housed Ansel's.

Its three stories were dark and forbidding in the rain; no light came from the rear, and the side that Kells could see seemed entirely windowless. It was raining hard by now—he rolled his coat collar up, pulled the brim of his soft hat down.

He slipped once in the mud, almost fell. In righting himself he remembered his wounded leg suddenly, sharply. It was throbbing steadily, swollen and hot with pain.

He went close to the building. It was very dark there, but looking up he could see the vague outline of a fire escape against the yellow glow of the sky. He smiled to himself in the darkness, put the back of his hand against his forehead. It was hot, dry.

He felt his way along the wall of the building until he was under the free-swinging end of the fire escape. It was almost four feet beyond his reach. He went back the way he had come to the fence, went along it until, in the corner the fence made with a squat outbuilding, he found a fairly large packing case. He stood on it and found that it would hold his weight; he balanced it on his shoulder and carried it back into the shadow of the building.

Standing on the box, he could just reach the end of the

159

fire escape; he put his weight on it, slowly. It creaked a little, came slowly down.

When the bottom step was resting on the packing case he crawled slowly, carefully up to the first landing. He lay on his side, held the free-swinging part so that it would come up quietly. Then he stood up.

Two windows gave on the second landing. One was boarded up snugly, no light came through. Kells put his ear to it, could hear only a confused hum of voices. The other window had been painted black on the inside but a long scratch ran diagonally across one of the panes. He took off his hat, put his eye close to the scratch.

He was looking into the office that ran almost the width of the building, was partitioned off from the big upstairs room by a wall of rough, unpainted pine boards.

The first person he saw was a woman whom he had never seen before. She was sitting on a broad desk, talking to two men. One of the men, in ill-fitting dinner clothes, was unfamiliar—the other man turned as he watched, and Kells recognized Lieutenant Reilly.

Reilly was heavy, shapeless. A cast in one eye gave his bloated, florid face a shrewdly evil quality. He was holding a tall glass of beer in one hand; he lifted it, drank deeply.

There were two large washtubs full of bottled beer and ice on the floor near the desk.

Another woman, in a bright orange evening gown, crossed Kells' line of vision, stooped and took two bottles from one of the tubs, disappeared.

Kells' lips framed the word. "Party." He was grinning.

Then he saw Ruth Perry. She was sitting on a dilapidated couch at one side of the room, swaying drunkenly back and forth, talking loudly to the man beside her. Kells put his ear to the pane but couldn't quite make out the words.

The man beside her was MacAlmon.

Then the rough pine door in the middle of the far wall opened and two men came in. In the moment the door was open, Kells saw a swirl of people around one of the crap tables in the big gambling room. Then the door closed; Kells looked at the two men.

One of them was a short-bodied, long-armed man whom

160

Kells remembered vaguely from somewhere. His face was broad and bland and child-like.

The other was Jack Rose.

Kells slid the big automatic out of its holster.

Rose's long, tanned, good-looking face was cheerful; his thin red mouth was curved to a smile. He crossed the room and sat down beside Ruth Perry, spoke across her to MacAlmon.

Kells looked thoughtfully down at the dark slippery steps beneath him. Looking down made him suddenly dizzy—he blinked, shook his head sharply, put one hand on the railing for support. He thought he was going to be sick for a moment, but the feeling passed. He was hot and the rain felt terribly cold on his head.

Then he looked up again, at the door. There was a big, planed two-by-four up and down its middle that could be swung sideways into two iron slots—one on each side of the door.

As he watched, the woman and Reilly and the other man whom he had seen first took up their glasses, went out of the room. That left—as nearly as he could judge—six or seven people. Rose, Ruth Perry, MacAlmon, the short man who had come in with Rose, the woman in the orange dress; perhaps two or three more whom he hadn't seen.

He looked at the crosspieces between the four panes of the window, felt their thickness with his fingers. Then he stood up and braced himself against the railing, released the safety on the automatic, put one foot against the crosspieces and pushed suddenly with all his weight. They gave way with a small splintering noise, glass tinkled on the floor. Kells stumbled on the lower part of the window frame, almost fell. He saved himself by grabbing the upper edge, felt a long sharp splinter of glass sink into the flesh of his hand. He held the automatic low, put one foot slowly down to the floor.

The woman in the orange dress looked as if she were going to scream; the man beside her took her arm suddenly, roughly—she put her free hand up to her mouth, was silent.

Rose had stood up; one hand was behind him. Kells jerked the automatic up in a savage gesture—Rose put his hands up slowly. Ruth Perry and MacAlmon were still sitting on the couch, and the short man was standing near them with his back to Kells, looking at Kells over his shoulder. The short man and MacAlmon put their hands up slowly.

Kells went swiftly sideways to the door, swung the bar. A great deal of noise came through the wall from the outer room and it occurred to him that perhaps the crashing of the window hadn't been heard outside.

Ruth Perry was staring blearily at Kells. She said: "Shay—whatch ish all about?"

MacAlmon put down one hand and put it over her mouth, said: "Shut up." MacAlmon was dead white.

Kells looked at the other man—the one he hadn't seen before, the one with the woman in the orange dress. He, too, put his hands up, rather more rapidly than the others had.

Someone pounded on the door, a voice shouted: "What's the matter in there?"

Kells looked at Rose. The automatic was rigid in his hand, focused squarely on Rose's chest.

Rose looked at the gun, swallowed.

MacAlmon said: "Nothing. . . ."

Rose swallowed again. He smiled weakly, licked his lips. "We're playing games."

There was laughter outside the door—a man's laughter and a woman's. The voice asked: "Post office?"

The woman in the orange dress giggled. Then her eyes rolled back in her head and she slumped down softly to the floor.

Ruth Perry pushed MacAlmon's hand away, stood up. She swayed, stared drunkenly at Kells; she shook her head sharply and staggered forward, said: "Well, 'm a dirty name—ish Gerry—good ol' son of a bitch, Gerry. Lesh have a drink." She stooped over one of the tubs, almost fell.

Kells was standing with his back to the door. His face was bloody and blood dripped from his cut left hand. He took a handkerchief out of his overcoat, held it to his face.

He said: "We'll take a walk, Jakie."

Rose moved his shoulders a little, half nodded.

Ruth Perry lost her balance, sprawled down on the floor.

She sat up slowly and leaned against the wall.

Kells was staring at Rose. His eyes were bright and cold and his mouth curved upward at the corners, ever so little. He said: "Come here."

Rose came across the room slowly. When he was close enough, Kells put his left hand on his shoulder suddenly, spun him around, slid his hand down to jerk a small caliber automatic out of Rose's hip pocket.

Kells said: "We're going out of here now. You're going to walk a little ahead of me, on my right. If we have any trouble, or if any of these gentlemen"—he jerked his head toward MacAlmon and the short man and the other man—"forget to sit still, I'm going to let your insides out on the floor."

He swung the bar up straight, took the key out of the door. "Do you understand?"

Rose nodded.

Ruth Perry staggered clumsily to her feet. She had picked up an ice pick that was lying by one of the tubs; she waved it at Kells. She said: "Don' go, Gerry—'s a swell party." She weaved unsteadily toward him.

Kells dropped Rose's gun into his left coat pocket, shifted his own gun to his left hand and shoved Ruth Perry away gently with his right.

She ducked suddenly under his outstretched arm, straightened up and brought her right hand around in a long arc hard against his back. The ice pick went in deep between his shoulder blades.

*   *   *   *   *

Kells stood very still for perhaps five seconds. Then he moved his head down slowly, looked at her.

Rose half turned and Kells straightened the automatic suddenly, viciously against his side. Rose put his hands a little higher, slowly lowered his head.

Ruth Perry was clinging to Kells with both arms. She had taken her hand away from the handle of the ice pick and her arms were around his waist, her face was pressed against his shoulder.

He moved the fingers of his right hand up into her hair and jerked her head back. She opened her eyes and looked up into his face; she was pale, white-lipped. Then she opened her mouth and threw her head back against his hand and laughed.

He smiled a little and took his hand from her hair, took his arm slowly from around her shoulder. He put his hand against her breast, pushed her gently away. She staggered back against the wall and slid slowly down to the floor; she lay there laughing and there was no sound but the sound of her laughter and the low buzz of voices outside.

Kells reached back with his right hand, pulled the ice pick halfway out. He swayed, leaned against the door a moment, jerked it the rest of the way out. It fell and stuck in the floor, the handle quivering.

He straightened then, swung the door partly open, stuck the automatic in his big overcoat pocket and said: "Let's go."

Rose put his hands down. He opened the door the rest of the way and went out of the room; Kells went out behind him and closed the door, said: "Wait a second."

Rose half turned, looked down at Kells' overcoat pocket. The muzzle of the automatic bulged the cloth.

Kells watched Rose, locked the door quickly with his left hand. They started down the long room together; Rose a pace to the right, a pace ahead.

There were perhaps thirty or thirty-five people—mostly men—in the room; most of them around the two crap tables, several at two small green-covered tables, drinking.

The lighting was as Kells remembered it: Two powerful shaded globes over the big tables lighting all the rear end of the room. Toward the front of the room—the street—the light faded to partial darkness, black in the far corners.

Kells said, "Talk to me, Jakie," out of the side of his mouth.

Rose turned his head and twisted his mouth to a terribly forced grin. His eyes were wide, frightened. "What'll I talk about?"

Several people turned to look at them.

Kells said: "The weather—an' walk faster."

Then someone crashed against the locked door behind them. In the same moment Kells saw Reilly. He had risen from one of the smaller tables, was staring at Rose.

He said: "Jack—what the hell? . . ."

Then he looked at Kells, his hand dipped toward his hip. Kells shot from his pocket—twice.

Reilly put his two hands against the middle of his chest, slowly. He sat down on the edge of the table, slid slowly down as his knees buckled, fell backward, half under the table.

Another gun roared and Kells felt the shoulder of his coat lift, tear; felt a hot stab in the muscle of his upper arm.

Rose was running toward the other end of the room, zigzagging a little, swiftly.

Kells started after him, stumbled, almost fell. He jerked the big automatic out of his pocket, swung it toward Rose. Then the door beyond Rose opened and someone came in. Kells couldn't see who it was; he staggered on after Rose, stopped suddenly as Rose stopped.

Borg said, "Cinch," out of the darkness.

Kells' gun roared and almost simultaneously another roared, flashed yellow out of the darkness near the door.

Rose's hands were together high in the air. He spun as though suspended by his hands from the ceiling, fell down to his knees, bent slowly forward.

Kells went to him swiftly and put the muzzle of the automatic against the back of his head and fired three times. He grunted, "Compliments Flo Beery," straightened and watched Rose topple forward, crush his dead face against the floor.

He turned to look toward the rear of the room and in that instant the two big lights went out, it was entirely black.

Borg's voice whispered beside him: "Oh, boy! Did I have a swell hunch when I turned off the lights in the little room outside—they could pick us off going out if I hadn't."

Borg led him to the door and they went across the little room in the darkness. Kells stumbled over something soft— Borg said: "I had to sap the doorman—he wasn't going to let me in."

Borg swung the heavy outer door wide and they went through to the stairs.

About halfway down Kells put his hand out suddenly and groped for the banister—his body pivoted slowly on one foot, crashed against the wall. He slid to his knees, still holding the banister tightly.

Borg put his hands under Kells' arms and locked them on his chest, tried to lift him.

Kells muttered something that sounded like, "Wait—minute," coughed.

Borg pried his hand off the banister, half dragged, half carried him the rest of the way downstairs.

It was raining very hard.

*　　*　　*　　*　　*

Kells straightened suddenly and pushed Borg away, said: "I'm all right." Then he leaned against the building and coughed, and the cough was a harsh, tearing sound deep inside him. He stood there coughing terribly until Borg dragged him away, shoved him into the car that had come swiftly to the curb.

Granquist was at the wheel. She said, "Well—hero!" sarcastically, as if she had been wanting to say that, thinking about saying that for a long time.

Kells' head sagged to her shoulder. There was blood on his mouth and his eyes were closed.

Borg climbed in behind him, closed the door.

Granquist threw her arms around Kells suddenly and pressed his head close against her shoulder. Her eyes were wide, stricken; her lower lip was caught between her teeth—she almost screamed: "Gerry—darling—for God's sake, say something!"

Borg was looking back through the side window at the dark archway that led to the stairs.

He said: "Let's get going."

Kells raised his head and opened his eyes. He waved an arm in the general direction of the car across the street—the car they had followed from Larson's.

Borg said: "We ain't got time to jim it up—besides, they got a flock of cars." He reached in front of Kells, shook Granquist, shouted: "Let's go."

She looked up blankly, then mechanically took her left arm from around Kells and grasped the wheel. She let the clutch in and the big coupé slid away from the curb.

"Duck down Gardner." Borg snapped on the dashlight, pulled Kells' overcoat and suit coat off his shoulder, ripped his shirt open and looked at the wound on the outer muscle of his left arm. "Crease," he said. Then he glanced through

166

the rear window, went on: "Turn right, here—no—the next one. This one's full of holes."

Granquist was bent over the wheel, staring intently through the dripping windshield. She jerked her head at Kells, asked: "Why's he coughing blood?" She spoke in a small, harsh, breathless voice.

Borg shrugged, went on examining Kells.

He glanced again through the rear window, said: "Here they come—give it everything."

They swung around a corner and the car leaped ahead, the engine throbbed, thundered. When Borg looked back again the headlights that marked the pursuing car were almost three blocks behind them.

He had bent Kells forward, was examining his back. He said: "He's bleeding like a stuck pig from a little hole in his back.

Wha' d' ya suppose done that?"

Kells straightened suddenly, sat up, struggled into his coat. He looked at Granquist, smiled faintly and put up one hand and rubbed it down his face. He said: "I guess I passed out—where we going?"

"Doctor's."

Kells said: "Don't be silly. We're going north—fast." He started coughing again, took out a handkerchief and held it to his mouth.

Borg said slowly: "I thought south—I guess I'm a lousy guesser."

"I told the cab driver who turned us in, north—they'll probably figure us for south—the Border." Kells spoke hoarsely, with a curious halting lisp. He leaned forward and began coughing again.

Granquist swung the car right, around another corner.

Borg was looking back. After a couple of blocks, he said: "I think we've lost 'em."

Kells sat up again as Granquist turned east on Sunset Boulevard. He said: "The other way, baby—the other way."

"We're going to a doctor's." She was almost crying.

Kells put his two hands forward and pulled the emergency brake back hard. The car skidded, turned half around, stopped.

Kells said, "Drive, Fat," wearily. He looked down at

Granquist, went on patiently: "Listen. We've got one chance in a hundred of getting away. Every police car and highway patrol in the county is looking for us by now. . . ."

Borg had opened the door, jumped out. He ran around the car and opened the other door and climbed in. Granquist and Kells moved over to make room for him.

Then, before Borg could close the door, a car bore down on them on Borg's side—a car without lights. Yellow-orange flame spurted from its side as it swerved sharply to avoid hitting them—Borg sank slowly forward over the wheel, sank slowly sideways, fell out the door into the street. The car was going too fast to stop suddenly—it went on toward the next corner, slowing. Flame spurted from its rear window; the windshield shattered, showered Kells and Granquist with glass.

Kells moved very swiftly. He crawled across Granquist, slammed the door shut, had flipped off the emergency and was headed west, in second, before the other car had turned around. He shifted to high, pressed the throttle to the floor.

Granquist was slumped low in the seat.

Kells glanced at her, asked: "You all right, baby?"

"Uh huh." She pressed close against him.

They went out Sunset at around seventy miles an hour, went on through Beverly Hills, on. At the ocean they turned north. The road was being repaired for a half-mile or so; Kells slowed to thirty-five.

Granquist had been watching through the rear window, had seen no sign of the other car. She was close against Kells and her arm was around his shoulders. Her eyes were wide, excited.

She kept saying: "Maybe we'll make it, darling—maybe we'll make it."

Kells started coughing again—Granquist held the wheel while he leaned against the door, coughed terribly, as if his lungs were being torn apart.

Rain swept in through the broken windshield.

Kells took the wheel again, said in a choked whisper: "I'll get a doctor in Ventura—if we get through." He stepped on the throttle until the needle of the speedometer quivered around seventy again.

There were very few cars on the road.

A little way beyond Topanga Canyon, Kells threw the car out of gear, jerked back the brake.

He said: "I guess you'd better drive. . . ."

Granquist helped him slide over in the seat, crawled across him to the wheel—they started again.

Kells leaned back in the corner, was silent.

As they neared the bridge south of Malibu, Granquist slowed a little. There was someone swinging a red lantern in the middle of the road. Then she pressed the throttle far down, veered sharply to the left past a car that was parked across the road.

She glanced back in a little while and saw its lights behind her, pressed the throttle to the floor.

The road curved a great deal. Granquist was bent forward over the wheel—the rain beat against her face; her eyes were narrowed to slits against the wind and the rain.

There was the faint sound of a shot, two, behind them, a metallic thud as a bullet buried itself somewhere in the body of the car.

Kells opened his eyes, turned to look back. He grinned at Granquist and his face was whiter than anything she had ever seen. He glanced ahead, said: "Give it hell, baby." Then he groped in his pocket, pulled out the big automatic. He smashed the glass of the rear window with the muzzle and rested the barrel on his forearm, sighted, fired.

He said, "Missed," swore softly.

He fired again, and as the car behind them swerved crazily off the road and stopped, said, "Bull's-eye," laughed soundlessly.

They passed two cars going the other way. Kells, looking back, saw one of them stop and start to turn around. Then they went around a curve and he couldn't see the car any more.

He glanced at the speedometer. "You'll have to do a little better. I think there's a fast one on our tail now."

She said: "The curves . . ."

"I know, baby—you're doing beautifully. Only a little faster." He smiled.

Granquist asked: "How's the cough?"

"Swell—I can't feel it any more." He patted his chest. "I feel a lot better."

She braced herself and used the brake hard as they went around a sharp curve.

"There's a pint of Bourbon in the side pocket. We got it from Jake back at the trick speakeasy. . . ."

Kells said: "My God! Why didn't you tell me about it before?" He reached for the bottle.

"I forgot. . . ."

She jerked the wheel suddenly, hard, screamed between clenched teeth.

Kells felt the beginning of the skid; he looked outward, forward into blackness. They were in space, falling sidewise into blackness; there was grinding, tearing, crashing sound. Falling. Black.

* * * * *

There was a light somewhere. There was a voice.

Kells moved his arm an inch or so, dug his fingers deep in mud. The rain beat hard, cold on his face.

The voice come from somewhere above him, kept talking about light.

"I can't get down any farther," it said. "We got to have more light."

Kells tried to roll over on his side. There was something heavy on his legs, he couldn't move them, couldn't feel them. But he twisted his body a little and opened his eyes. It was entirely dark.

He twisted his body the other way and saw the narrow beam of a flashlight high above him in the darkness. The rain looked like snow in the light.

He pushed himself up slowly, leaned on one elbow, saw something white a little distance away. He got his legs, somehow, out of the dark sharp metal that imprisoned them and crawled slowly, painfully toward the whiteness.

The whiteness was Granquist. She was dead.

Kells lay there awhile in the mud, on his belly, with his face close to Granquist's face.

He could not think. He could feel the awful, barbed pain in his body; after a while, fear. He looked up at the light and a wave of panic swept suddenly over him, twisted his heart. He wanted to go into the darkness, away from the light. He wanted the darkness very much.

He kissed Granquist's cold mouth and turned and crawled through the mud away from the light, away from the voices.

He wanted to be alone in the darkness; he wanted the light to please go away.

He whispered, "Please go away," to himself, over and over.

The ground was rough; great rocks jutted out of the mud, and there were little gullies that the rain had made.

After a while he stopped and turned and looked back and he could not see the light any more. Still he crawled on, dragged his torn body over the broken earth.

In the partial shelter of a steep sloping rock he stopped, sank forward, down.

There, after a little while, life went away from him.

Paul Cain is a pseudonym for George Carroll Syms, who was born in Des Moines, Iowa, in 1902. He wrote screenplays under the name of Peter Ruric. He is the author of one novel, *Fast One,* and one short-story collection, *Seven Slayers.*